GIRL SEVEN:

CRAVED

(A Maya Gray FBI Suspense Thriller—Book 7)

Molly Black

Molly Black

Bestselling author Molly Black is author of the MAYA GRAY FBI suspense thriller series, comprising nine books (and counting); of the RYLIE WOLF FBI suspense thriller series, comprising six books (and counting); of the TAYLOR SAGE FBI suspense thriller series, comprising eight books (and counting); of the KATIE WINTER FBI suspense thriller series, comprising eleven books (and counting); and of the RUBY HUNTER FBI suspense thriller series, comprising three books (and counting).

An avid reader and lifelong fan of the mystery and thriller genres, Molly loves to hear from you, so please feel free to visit www.mollyblackauthor.com to learn more and stay in touch.

ISBN: 978-1-0943-7830-5

BOOKS BY MOLLY BLACK

MAYA GRAY MYSTERY SERIES

GIRL ONE: MURDER (Book #1)
GIRL TWO: TAKEN (Book #2)
GIRL THREE: TRAPPED (Book #3)
GIRL FOUR: LURED (Book #4)
GIRL FIVE: BOUND (Book #5)
GIRL SIX: FORSAKEN (Book #6)
GIRL SEVEN: CRAVED (Book #7)
GIRL EIGHT: HUNTED (Book #8)
GIRL NINE: GONE (Book #9)

RYLIE WOLF FBI SUSPENSE THRILLER

FOUND YOU (Book #1)
CAUGHT YOU (Book #2)
SEE YOU (Book #3)
WANT YOU (Book #4)
TAKE YOU (Book #5)
DARE YOU (Book #6)

TAYLOR SAGE FBI SUSPENSE THRILLER

DON'T LOOK (Book #1)
DON'T BREATHE (Book #2)
DON'T RUN (Book #3)
DON'T FLINCH (Book #4)
DON'T REMEMBER (Book #5)
DON'T TELL (Book #6)
DON'T HIDE (Book #7)
DON'T BLINK (Book #8)

KATIE WINTER FBI SUSPENSE THRILLER

SAVE ME (Book #1)
REACH ME (Book #2)
HIDE ME (Book #3)
BELIEVE ME (Book #4)
HELP ME (Book #5)
FORGET ME (Book #6)
HOLD ME (Book #7)
PROTECT ME (Book #8)

REMEMBER ME (Book #9)
CATCH ME (Book #10)
WATCH ME (Book #11)

RUBY HUNTER FBI SUSPENSE THRILLER
IF I RUN (Book #1)
IF I TELL (Book #2)
IF I LIVE (Book #3)

CHAPTER ONE

When Hank heard a group of people coming towards him, he scuttled into one of Lagoon City's alleys. He didn't want trouble. The last thing he needed was to walk into the midst of a group of stragglers coming back after a drunken night out that had lasted until dawn. He'd learned the hard way that some people saw nothing wrong with beating up a man like him just for the fun of it. He had no wish to get kicked into the gutter, just for someone else's amusement.

He had never much liked Lagoon City, in spite of living there most of his life. The lakes nearby meant mist coming in, making the early morning light into something weak and diffuse, making him feel like he was walking through rain even though it promised to be a pleasant day. It lent a sheen to the t-shirt and cheap army surplus jacket he was wearing, and slicked back his tangled, unkempt hair.

Hank didn't like to think of himself as down and out, more sort of existing in between things. Between jobs, between places to stay, between girlfriends. Also somewhere carefully between the right side of the law and outright criminality, most days. He found what he needed out on the city's streets, whether that was money, food, or alcohol, and so long as no one looked too closely at exactly how he found those things, everything was fine. He worked small grifts, he took whatever wasn't watched too closely, no one got hurt. Currently, he was making his way back towards the squat he was staying in at the moment, after a night spent… well, he didn't remember half of it, but he assumed that it had been fun.

Once he was sure he was away from the people who had come too close, he strolled almost casually along the streets of the city, moving without a care because this time of the morning, when it was all just waking up, was his favorite time of day. There weren't too many people out yet. All the tourists heading to the lakes to fish or canoe or whatever were still in bed. All the folks who ran stores weren't ready to open up yet. He had the streets mostly to himself.

Thankfully, he knew most of the back alleys of the city, all the ones off the pristine streets that were kept that way just so that the tourists who came there for the lakes would feel good. He knew the ones that were the favorite spots for dealers, the ones that were best not to set foot in unless you wanted trouble.

The alley he slipped into next wasn't one of those. It was the kind of alley that people could use as a shortcut safely, back behind a restaurant and a row of houses. Hank made his way along it quickly, the sensation of wanting the streets to himself giving way to wanting to get back home. He passed by a dumpster…

That was when he saw the woman lying there at the side of the alley, face down in the dirt.

She was young and blonde, wearing a white dress that was stained now from lying there in the street. One of her shoes had come off and was resting a little way away, looking somehow as if it told the whole story of the night.

For a moment or two, Hank thought that maybe she was just passed out drunk. Maybe worth checking the purse near her for a wallet, but other than that best to leave her alone. He didn't want the kind of trouble that might come if she woke up with him standing over her.

Then he saw the length of braided cord around her neck and started to take in the unnatural stillness as she lay there. There was no rise and fall of her chest, none of the small twitches that most drunks made in their sleep.

Horror crept through Hank as he realized that this woman was dead. Someone had killed her. Someone had strangled her. Someone had *murdered* her.

And he was standing right next to the body. If someone came along now, they wouldn't stop to ask any questions; they would just assume that it was him. Even the cops would assume it was him because he'd had enough run-ins with them in the past that it would just be an easy story for them to tell. The street hustler who had gone too far. It would be an open and shut case for them.

Hank had to get out of there. He turned, not exactly to run, because that would attract attention that he didn't need, but certainly walk away as quickly as possible. As he did so, a flicker of something caught his eye, something that shone brightly and stopped him in his tracks.

Hank saw the small gemstone sitting there, left by the woman's body as casually as if it didn't matter at all. Simple avarice stopped Hank from walking away as he knew he should, making him stare at it. Something like that… if he could find a way to sell it safely, it could set him up, earn him enough to live on for… well, he didn't want to guess how long for, but a while.

He knew he ought to leave it there with the body; something like that could bring him all kinds of trouble. Even so, his hand shot out almost automatically, grabbing for it. He couldn't help himself when it came to this kind of thing. He couldn't just leave something like that *behind*, any more than he could keep from conning a mark or lifting a wallet.

He couldn't just leave the body, either. Hank might be a grifter, but there were some things you didn't do. He kept a burner phone for some of his cons, and because sometimes he did small jobs for people that needed anonymity. It was paid for in cash, with no way to trace it back to him. Getting out his phone, he did something he'd never thought he'd do and called 911.

"911, what service do you need?"

"Listen," Hank said. "I just found a body, in an alley off West Street."

"Could you repeat that please?"

"A body, off West Street."

"And what's your name?"

"That's not important," Hank said, and hung up as quickly as he could. He didn't want to give them any time to trace the call. He didn't want to get involved. He'd done what he had to do, and he had the stone to show for it. No one would ever know that he'd taken it, or that he was even here. No one was around, and no one would know that the stone was ever there.

Grabbing the stone, he hurried through the alley, wanting to put as much distance between himself and the dead woman as possible.

CHAPTER TWO

"You're my sister, not my mother."

Maya found herself thinking back to the last time she'd talked to her sister Megan.

"I just want to make sure you're ok. Going off traveling at random..."

"It's not random. It's something I need to do. I need to work out what I'm doing next. Maybe art college."

Maya had let the argument go, let her sister go. She'd assumed that there would be more time. She'd been so busy with her job that she'd let things drift with Megan. When she disappeared, Maya hadn't even noticed at first.

That was one of the biggest regrets of Maya's life, only made worse by the fact that Megan was currently in the hands of the Moonlight Killer, a truly deadly serial killer whose actual tally of kills even Maya didn't know.

She had to catch him. She had to find him, and her sister.

Currently Maya was at home, in her largely featureless D.C. apartment. Maya sat at the heart of the apartment, in the small, deliberately bland lounge area that lay next to her home gym, and stared at the evidence board she'd set up in one corner where she could take it all in.

She didn't want to think about what she would look like to anyone who came in. She was tall and dark-haired, still sweaty from a workout on the punchbag designed to take out some of her frustrations, and wearing gray sweats that were a little baggy on her. The combination of all that with the evidence board and a series of FBI files set out around her would probably make her look like some unkempt crazy woman to anyone who saw her.

Not that anyone would. If there was one thing Maya had in her apartment, it was a sense of solitude. Even security.

At least, she used to have it. The Moonlight Killer had managed to erode even that with his intrusions into her life, leaving postcards at her door with demands that had to be met or he would kill one of the women he called his "bunnies."

Maya focused on the pictures of those women, set up on her evidence board, hoping that simply staring would somehow give her more, let her see some hint of a connection there that might help her to get to their captor.

She already had one piece of information, of course, one link between the women whose names she knew: they'd all been on the verge of some big moment of change in their lives. They'd all been about to transform, through chance or choice, into something new. There were artists and singers up there on the verge of their big breaks, women who were trying to change careers, one woman who had just managed to get sober.

Maya had seen the pattern, seen that the Moonlight Killer was robbing them of their chance to be different when he'd kidnapped them. Now, she found herself going through other cases, the ones that weren't kidnappings, looking at the stack of murders attributed to him to see if the same pattern might apply.

There were so many of them by now that it was hard to wade through them all. Especially when there was a dedicated Moonlight Killer taskforce already, headed by Agent Swift of the FBI, who would probably ask difficult questions if she found out that Maya was accessing the Moonlight Killer files too often. Maya had the excuse that the "unknown kidnapper" was making her pursue cases with a Moonlight Killer connection, but if anyone found out the truth that the kidnapper *was* the Moonlight Killer…

That would be bad. Very bad, and not just for her career. Her sister's life could be at stake.

Maya had no doubt that if her boss, Agent Harris, found out that the kidnapper and the Moonlight Killer were one and the same, he would immediately disband the small task force Maya now headed up, taking away any autonomy she possessed in her investigations. He would go all out to try to force a conclusion to this, sending as many men as it took to catch the Moonlight Killer, not caring how many of the remaining hostages died in the process. He would reason that catching one of the country's most dangerous serial killers was worth even that sacrifice.

Maya couldn't allow that. She suspected that it wouldn't even work. The Moonlight Killer had been ahead of them at every step. In the face of an attempt to capture him, he would kill his hostages and simply disappear.

That was why she'd done everything she could to keep the information from Harris. Only she and her partner Marco Spinelli knew, a situation that might well cost both of them their jobs or more if the information came out. It was a dangerous piece of information to hold back, one she was sure Harris would say could be vital in trying to catch the Moonlight Killer, but Maya didn't see it like that. Just knowing the identity of the kidnapper didn't make it any easier to actually catch him. If anything, it would mean Harris blundering in with the aid of Agent Reyes, his would be protégé, making so many ripples while they did it that they would scare the Moonlight Killer into killing his hostages and disappearing again, for good this time.

Maya's approach was the only way to do this. It was the only way to both get the hostages back and try to catch the Moonlight Killer. Alone, in control of the situation, making sure that nothing went wrong.

That thought brought a wave of frustration with it, one that had her standing and going back to the punchbag she kept hanging in her home gym. Maya threw on bag gloves, moving around it, throwing jabs and crosses as hard as she could, every impact trying to shake loose some of that frustration.

Thud, thud.

Maya hit hard enough to hurt her hands even through the gloves, but the punches didn't do anything to help her current state of mind, though. The fact was that she *wasn't* in control. The Moonlight Killer was. He sent her postcards and she jumped to do whatever he told her to.

Thud, thud. Thwack.

Maya put in a Thai style round kick with her shin, turning her hip all the way over so that the impact against the bag reverberated through her leg, not that it made things any better. No amount of training did. As much as she worked and sweated, it didn't make a real difference to her situation. It couldn't erase thoughts of the Moonlight Killer and Megan from her mind.

She was stuck like a bug, caught in a web of the Moonlight Killer's creation, trying to understand enough about him to get to the truth before his plans got Maya or her sister killed.

Maya stepped back from the bag. It wasn't making any difference to the way she felt. Only catching the Moonlight Killer and saving her sister would do that.

Thankfully, Maya had one thing that might help more with that. Able to move again now from the bag, she went to her computer, trying to do some basic research. She kept her phone well away from her while she did it, face down in a drawer in the kitchen. Maya knew without a doubt that the Moonlight Killer had been listening in on her calls and she wasn't sure if that level of observation ran to passively listening to everything around the phone as well. Maya couldn't risk him finding out anything about what she was going to do next.

She had one piece of information that had nothing to do with the connections between the women, one piece that had come from her sister Megan, passed on by the last woman Maya had managed to save by solving one of the mysteries the Moonlight Killer had sent her to unravel. Tori had whispered the words in her ear even as Maya had pulled her from under the buoy where the Moonlight Killer had hidden her.

"Megan says that she heard saw-whet owls."

It was a small piece of information, but maybe it would be enough to get her closer. It was also information that Maya had decided not to pass on to Agent Harris, knowing that he would only dive headfirst into another of the raids that had endangered so many lives before. Maya needed to hold this information back, keep it to herself until she could find a way to use it that would actually capture the killer.

Did it mean anything that Megan had heard the bird? That was one of the things that Maya needed to work out. The Moonlight Killer had laid false trails before, controlling what his captives saw and smelled so that fragments of evidence they provided proved to lead the FBI into traps he had set specifically to catch out those breaking the rules of his sick game. Even Maya had been caught out by it before, and it had cost his captives.

Was this another case like that? Was it another temptation to break the Moonlight Killer's rules?

It was possible, but Maya dared to hope that it wasn't this time. Megan must know the kind of man who held her and the others hostage by now. She had to know that he might play tricks, so she would only pass on something that she felt might be real.

Maya had to trust her little sister's judgement on this. *Especially* given the content. Maya knew about birds. Spotting them while out hiking had always been something she'd enjoyed doing as a kid, but it wasn't something she'd done a lot of in recent years, or at least, she hadn't put anything about it on her social media. There was no way, as far as Maya could see, for the Moonlight Killer to know that Maya would be able to recognize the bird call. It wasn't something he had any reason to set up to trick her with.

That made it more likely that it was real and, in turn, that meant that Maya had to take it seriously. If her sister was taking the risk to send her the information, then Maya had to hope that it was valuable. She started to look up the saw-whet owl on her computer, but at first glance, it didn't seem to tell her much. This was just a particularly small example of an owl, one that was pretty common in some places. Maya wasn't sure how it helped to narrow things down.

Then she started looking for it in Virginia, because everything she'd seen so far suggested that the Moonlight Killer was based somewhere there. He was close enough that he could move women to release them there quickly, while none of the women who had been rescued after Maya solved a case had talked about traveling long distances across the country, even though they hadn't been able to see where they'd come from. He had to be holding them close by, or those facts simply didn't fit.

Looking at the saw-whet owl in the context of Virginia did a lot to narrow down the results.

There seemed to be only a few small clusters of them in the state, each breeding pair sticking to well established territories. Megan obviously knew that or she wouldn't have thought that the information was important to pass on to her. Maya got out a map and started to mark them out, drawing small red circles in every spot they were known to be found.

She found herself both encouraged by being able to narrow down the search area a little but also still slightly frustrated. The information Megan had given her wasn't quite enough to warrant just searching each of those areas for a probable spot where the Moonlight Killer was holding her. It certainly wasn't something that Maya and Marco would be able to do between them, yet if they called in the full resources of the FBI to help, it would simply be too obvious. The Moonlight Killer would hear what was happening long before they found the location and that would only put Megan in danger.

Maya felt sick at the thought of her sister in his hands, helpless to stop him from hurting her. He'd already beaten her systematically once when Maya hadn't managed to stop a raid from going ahead, sending her pictures of every injury he inflicted. If he found out about this, Maya had no doubt that he would do far worse.

A part of her suspected that he was never going to let her sister go, whatever Maya did. He was releasing other women as Maya solved cases, but of course he was holding Megan until last. Would he release her then? What if Maya failed to solve even one of the cases he set for her? Would Megan be the one to pay the price then? A part of Maya felt certain that he was just looking for an excuse to make her feel that pain by killing her sister.

Maya was still considering the full horror of that possibility when Marco called.

"Hey, Marco," Maya said. It was impossible to keep from smiling as she picked up the phone. She hadn't anticipated just how close the two of them would get, the kiss they'd shared on their last case the culmination of so much for the two of them over the course of their last few cases. "Please tell me you're not calling to cancel our date."

"That part's up to you," Marco said. "But I just had news that might make you want to reconsider."

That sounded ominous, sending a worm of worry digging its way into Maya. "What news?"

"There's been a report of a woman killed on the full moon in D.C. She was strangled."

"You think it was the Moonlight Killer's work?"

"*I* don't know what to think, but Swift and her team have claimed the case as theirs, so *they* obviously think that it is. They're pushing out anyone else who wants to look at it."

"Including you?" Maya asked. If the Moonlight Killer had truly struck again, especially so close by, then what did that mean? Maya had assumed that he would be busy with the game he was playing with her. This seemed to suggest something else. Was he getting bored of making her dance to his tune? If so, was her sister in danger of him simply giving up on his game?

"I managed to grab some information," Marco said. "A few basic details, at least. I thought maybe we could talk it over at lunch."

That took Maya a little aback. "Aren't you worried about this ending up like our first date?"

On that date, what seemed like an eternity ago, Maya had been so worried about what was happening with her sister that she hadn't been able to talk about anything else. It didn't help that she'd drunk too much to try to cope with the stress of it all, either. The whole evening had been a disaster. About as far from a real date as it was possible to get.

"I've decided that I need to accept you just as you are," Marco said. "If that includes talking work in the middle of a lunch date, then I guess that's just the price we both have to pay."

Maya wished that she could just say no to talking about the case, but she knew that her mind wouldn't be able to focus on anything else now that she'd heard the news. It would make for a far *worse* date with her being distracted the whole time than if the two of them just acknowledged that they both had an interest in trying to catch the Moonlight Killer.

"Bring whatever you have," Maya said. "But still dress up. We're still going to make a date of this if it kills us."

"I always dress up!" Marco insisted, but Maya caught the note of amusement there in his voice.

"In a sports jacket and jeans, most of the time," Maya countered. He was a long way from being the neatest person Maya had met. It was just one of the things that Maya liked about him.

"All right, but if I have to, you have to."

"I'm planning on it. See you there."

Maya hung up. She had to go shower, and not just because she had a date to get to. The sooner she got there, the sooner she could find out what was going on with the Moonlight Killer.

Just the thought of the killer made her skin crawl. She wanted to catch him more than ever now. Maya resented him even more for intruding on this part of her life, but she wasn't going to let this go. If there was anything more to learn here, maybe it would lead to her sister.

CHAPTER THREE

When she arrived at the restaurant, only a few minutes late, Maya had to admit that Marco's attempts to dress up suited him.

He was standing by one of the tables, wearing a dark blue suit that she hadn't known he owned. It fit him well, hugging his tall swimmer's body, with a white shirt and no tie, because even if dressing up, there was no way that Marco was going to wear a tie. His dark hair was more neatly clipped than usual, framing chiseled, handsome features that it was hard for Maya to tear her eyes away from as she made her way over to the table.

Maya had made her own effort at dressing up for the date in a simple dark dress with a cream colored coat thrown over her shoulders, her dark hair allowed to spill down for once rather than keeping it tied back professionally. She hoped that it was enough to match Marco's efforts. She'd also left her phone at home. She had no wish to let the Moonlight Killer listen in on their date.

The restaurant wasn't anything fancy, partly because neither of them would have been comfortable with that and partly because of how badly things had gone the last time they'd tried for a date. There were a few diners inside with it being lunchtime, but there was still plenty of space around, too. That was good because it would make talking about murder easier. Maya had learned a long time ago that normal people didn't talk about that kind of thing over their dinner, and gave her strange looks if she was the one doing it.

"You look amazing," Marco said as Maya got closer to him. Maya was tall, but at well over six feet, Marco was taller. It left Maya looking up at him, with the urge to lean in and kiss him almost overwhelming.

Maya managed to turn it into a kiss on his cheek, because she suspected that making out wasn't quite the normal way of opening a lunch date. It would have looked strange to the people at the other tables. It was better to save it for afterwards.

"You don't look so bad yourself," she said with a smile. Seeing Marco always made her feel better in spite of the pressure she was under with the Moonlight Killer cases.

She sat with him, the two of them ordering. Marco had the steak; Maya chose the fish. She didn't order any wine, both because it was only lunchtime and because of the way she'd overdone it the last time they'd gone out for a meal together. Maya had been so distracted by thoughts of her sister's captivity that she hadn't been able to focus on anything else.

Now, Maya made an effort not to do that. She didn't want this to turn out the same way. They were out on a date together; it didn't seem right to dive straight into work, somehow. Maya tried to think of something else to talk about first. Anything at all that wasn't the case.

"How are things with your family back in Cleveland?" Maya asked. It was a dull question, just small talk of the kind that she and Marco were well past by now. They'd saved one another's lives, going after some of the most dangerous criminals out there.

"Aren't you going to ask me about the woman who was found dead?" Marco countered, looking at Maya carefully, as if seeing something there that no one else would have. Maybe he was trying to judge why she was trying to make small talk.

"It didn't feel like a suitable thing to talk about on a date," Maya said. "At least not to open with."

Marco reached out to touch her hand. That contact was electric, but the suddenness of it was a slight surprise. Not a bad surprise, though. Far from it. Maya wanted to lean into his touch, enjoying every moment of contact she could get with him. She wanted to linger there.

"Maya, I told you on the phone, I'm ok with talking work. It's this huge part of both of our lives, so it would be pretty strange if we *didn't* talk about it. Especially now, given what's happened."

Maya got that; she just didn't want it to feel as if she was only there with Marco because of the case they were working together. She wanted to be there with him because of *him,* and how much she liked him. She was there on a date with him because she liked him and wanted to spend that time with him. She'd wanted to get closer to him pretty much since the first moment she met him. It was just that things had always gotten in the way. Was it wrong to want a brief moment just for the two of them?

"We're both in law enforcement," Marco said. "We're partners as well as… well, whatever this is. We should be in a place where we can talk over work together even like this. What's the alternative? We sit here and talk about… I don't know, baseball?"

"Do you *like* baseball?" Maya asked him. She realized that she didn't even know that much about him, because most of the things she'd learned had been about his capacity to bring in bad guys. There were whole facets of his life that she didn't know enough about right now.

"Guardians all the way," Marco replied, with an almost boyish grin that made him, if anything, even more handsome. Of course that would be his team since he was from Cleveland. "Seriously, though, ask me what we both know you want to ask."

Maya gave in. As much as they were both on a date, there were things that she needed to know.

"What did you find out about the dead woman?" Maya asked, now that he'd said it was ok to ask. It was impossible *not* to ask it, when the answer might bring the two of them closer to the man they'd been hunting together for so long now. "They're treating it as a Moonlight Killer murder?"

Marco nodded. "Which makes it difficult to find out too much, because Agent Swift's taskforce has claimed it as their own. I managed to get a look at the files, though. The deceased is a woman named Cassandra Moore, worked as a PI."

That seemed like an odd choice of victim for the Moonlight Killer, given when Maya thought she knew about his motivations. It didn't seem like the kind of person who would fit his usual pattern.

"Is there any sign that she was on the verge of changing careers, or maybe changing her whole life in some way?" Maya asked. That was the MO she'd been working with so far. If this didn't fit, what did it mean?

Marco shrugged. "I only have what I got from a quick glance at the files, plus a little research I was able to do on her. As far as I can see, she was in her job a while, but there's something about her business that's just a bit…"

"A bit what?" Maya asked. She'd learned to trust Marco's instincts on some things, and this was one of them. Where she'd spent her time in the FBI working cold cases, developing the skills to find fresh evidence in files that seemed dusty and dead, Marco had been a cop back in Cleveland, a detective working homicide. It had left him with a knowledge of the way bad guys worked on the streets that Maya couldn't match.

Marco spread his hands, obviously trying to find the right way to put it. "You meet a few PIs as a cop. Mostly doing divorce work, or gathering evidence for someone's law firm, you know?"

It didn't come up so much with cold cases, but Maya got the general idea. Occasionally there had been a PI involved back in an old case. She nodded, knowing that he understood PIs and how they operated.

"But there are always some who are shadier. Ones who are PIs or 'security consultants' because 'hitman' doesn't look so good as a job description, ones who get involved in corporate espionage, ones who are into blackmail…"

"You think Cassandra Moore was dirty?" Paige asked him. She saw Marco nod. "But that might mean… what if she's one of the people who has been helping the Moonlight Killer with the stuff around the kidnappings? With following us, delivering those postcards, all of it?"

He'd been using people like that, because the way he was surveilling them was simply too much for one man to pull off alone. Especially when he had to keep watch over his captives to make sure that none of them had a chance to escape.

Marco was silent for a few seconds. "We don't have any proof of that, but yes, it might fit."

In Maya's mind, the possibility fit perfectly. So perfectly that she had a hard time believing that it could be anything else. They already knew that the Moonlight Killer used people to do his bidding; just look at what he was doing with her. He couldn't be everywhere at once, so he needed people to be his eyes and ears, to do his dirty work at a distance. He had them deliver postcards for him, track people down, watch them. Who better for that kind of work than a PI who seemed shady to Marco's experienced eye?

"Which begs the question of why he would kill her," Maya said. "Unless… maybe she found out something that she shouldn't. Something about him. You know how guarded he is about secrecy."

"You're thinking that if we look into Cassandra Moore, we might find something that could lead back to him," Marco guessed.

Maya nodded, feeling a hint of hope at the thought. More than a hint. If Cassandra Moore really had found out something, then maybe it was the break they needed. They needed to know more.

"There are a couple of things in the way," Marco pointed out. "First, he's careful. He doesn't leave traces that could be followed back to him."

"So far," Maya countered.

"Second, it isn't our investigation. We can't just walk in and demand to see everything on Cassandra Moore, because Agent Swift's people will want to know why."

And they couldn't tell them why, not without putting Megan in danger.

"We can find a way," Maya insisted. "Maybe we can go to the local PD to get the information directly."

"Without Harris noticing?" Marco asked. "Besides, there's the third reason, which is that we don't know for sure that Cassandra Moore knew anything, or even that this was down to the Moonlight Killer."

"It's him," Maya said, even though there wasn't any evidence to back up her hunch. She wanted it to be him, though. She *needed* it to be him. If it was, then there was at least a chance of finding something that might help them, something that might get them closer to the truth.

Marco's hand squeezed hers. The pressure of the gesture was familiar, comforting, and reminded Maya of just how close the two of them were starting to get to one another. It felt easy for her to simply be here like this with Marco, just the two of them on something that was half-date and half-work, pitched in a space that was all their own. Maybe that was the way things needed to be for them. It seemed obvious from their attempts at dates so far that they would never be the kind of couple that just did ordinary romantic things together. Trying to catch bad guys was a big part of who they both were, so maybe it should be a part of who they were as a couple as well.

Were they a couple, though? They'd kissed, but it had been in the aftermath of a high stress situation where they'd both been in danger. They'd been on dates, but work and the threat to Maya's sister always found a way to intrude. Was that enough?

Was it even a good idea to let anyone get close to her when there was a serial killer embroiled in her life? It was obvious that the Moonlight Killer was playing a twisted game with her, and that he wouldn't hesitate to hurt the people around her. Getting closer to Marco might only put him in danger, giving the Moonlight Killer more reason to hurt him.

Did he *need* a reason to hurt Marco, though, and should Maya be making decisions about her personal life based on what a serial killer might or might not do? Both of those questions hung inside Maya's head, not going away.

"Are you all right, Maya?" Marco could obviously see some reflection of those thoughts on Maya's face.

"I'm fine," she assured him.

"Are you sure?" Marco asked. "You look troubled."

Maya wasn't sure what to say to that. She certainly couldn't tell him everything that she'd been thinking, because that would only make things far too complicated between them, would put too many obstacles in their way. But now that Marco was pushing the point, she also knew that she couldn't just tell him that she was fine again, or he would only keep pushing to find out more.

For an instant, she was grateful when one of the wait staff there came over, the young woman looking both puzzled and slightly determined. Maya didn't understand for a second or two what she was doing there. Maybe to see if they wanted wine? Then Maya saw the rectangle of cardboard gripped carefully in her right hand, held out towards Maya, obviously intended for her.

"Are you Agent Gray?" the young woman asked. "A courier came. He said that this was for you. He said it was urgent."

Maya looked around quickly, trying to catch any glimpse of a courier. As always when it came to this, though, there wasn't anyone there, no sign of anyone she could question about all this. Instead, all she could do was reach out to take the postcard from the young woman's hand, setting it down in the middle of the table.

A familiar bunny design stared back at Maya, in this case a collection of hand drawn bunnies gamboling happily in a field. There was nothing happy about the presence of it there, though, because of what it meant.

The Moonlight Killer had sent her another postcard. He had another job for her to do.

CHAPTER FOUR

Maya flipped over the postcard, determined to find out what the Moonlight Killer wanted from her this time.

At least, a part of her *hoped* that he wanted something because the alternative was significantly worse. If this wasn't a demand for her to solve a case, then it might be him telling her that one of the women he'd captured had died, or that he'd chosen to kill one of them because he felt the FBI had overstepped in some way.

It might mean that he'd decided to crush her by killing Megan then telling her about it.

That prospect meant that there was a rising hint of terror in Maya as she started to read.

Dear Maya,

It's time for you to show what you can do again. Reba Andrews, Lagoon City. I am not feeling generous today. Three days. Midnight.

Maya felt a wave of relief that she wasn't reading the news that her sister had been killed, mixed in with a sudden awareness that she needed to do something, needed to act now in response to the demand that the Moonlight Killer had just made of her.

Three days wasn't long. It wasn't *enough.* Maya had solved cases quickly before, but that wasn't how cold cases were meant to work. The one advantage of a case being cold was meant to be that it gave her enough time to run things down properly, working through the evidence little by little. The pressure that the Moonlight Killer applied to her took away that time, forcing her to try to find answers at a speed that shouldn't have been possible.

The only advantages she possessed were the knowledge that he sent her out on cases where it had been wrongly assumed that he was involved, and the fact that Marco was there beside her.

"We have to get to Lagoon City," Maya said. She was already halfway out of her seat. "I'll need to rush home to grab a bag, then I'll meet you at the airport. I'll call Samit to get us whatever details he can, and to book us some flights, then-"

"Maya, breathe," Marco said. He stood with her, putting both of his hands on her shoulders to hold her in place. On another occasion, Maya might have thought that he was about to lean in for a kiss. "You're going too fast."

"We *have* to move fast," Maya countered. "We only have three days and we have a murder to solve, we're going to need every moment we can get."

She tried to make it sound like she was being proactive, trying to get this done because the unsolved case demanded it. She tried to tell herself that she was doing this for the victims, for justice, to stop a killer who desperately needed to be stopped. She tried to tell herself that this was just what she would have done if she had heard about this case any other way.

The problem with that was that Maya knew the truth: the Moonlight Killer was a spider and she was dancing helplessly in his web, doing exactly what he required of her while trying to pretend that she had some kind of choice in it. She had no choice; she either did what he wanted or her sister died. He had complete control over her.

"We'll solve this," Marco said. "But there's moving quickly and then there's rushing. First thing, we don't need to book flights. I'm pretty sure that Lagoon City is about an hour and a half's drive from here. Second, we need to pay the bill here before we run off. Third, you need to take the time to relax and think all of this through if we're actually going to find any answers. So how about I meet you back at your place after you've grabbed your stuff, then we drive down there, and you can try to catch up on the case on the way?"

It was a good plan, and once again, Maya found herself more than grateful that Marco was there with her. The two of them still needed to move quickly though, so she found herself hurrying towards the exit to the restaurant and her waiting car. She needed to get home.

Maya drove home as quickly as she dared without attracting the attention of any D.C. traffic cops. She might be going quickly in the course of a case, but the last thing she wanted right then was the kind of delay that might result from being pulled over, especially if news of it might reach Agent Harris's ears. Maya might be in charge of her own task force thanks to the pressure she'd been able to exert on her boss, but that wouldn't stop Harris from demanding answers, especially when he heard that there was a new case.

Reaching her apartment, Maya grabbed the bag she kept packed for exactly this kind of thing, throwing on a simple dark suit to travel in. She made sure that she had her gun, badge, and cuffs, then threw her laptop on top of the bag and got out her phone.

Maya called Samit, the tech who had been assigned to her small taskforce and who had proven to be invaluable so far. He picked up quickly.

"Agent Gray, I wasn't expecting to hear from you on your day off," he said.

"There's been another postcard." The seriousness of Maya's tone must have gotten through to him because his own response was swift and professional.

"What do you need?"

Maya appreciated that. There wasn't any time to lose at this point.

"I need you to send me over any files you can find on the death of Reba Andrews in Lagoon City. See what you can find out about her online presence, too. Send everything to my laptop."

"You're on your way there now?" Samit asked.

"That's right."

"Then I'll also book you and Marco hotel rooms and see if I can get through to local law enforcement to let them know that you're coming."

Maya smiled at the efficiency with which he was handling the situation. Marco might be her partner, but Samit was always there somewhere in the background, making sure that the two of them had what they needed. Without him, their last couple of cases wouldn't have gone anywhere near as smoothly.

"Thanks, Samit."

"What should I tell Agent Harris?" Samit asked.

"I'll let him know about the case once we're on our way," Maya replied. She didn't want to put her tech in her boss's line of fire, but she also didn't want to let Harris know too much about what was going on too early. She wished that she could say that she trusted her boss, but he'd proven time and again that his decisions were likely to put her sister in danger. Maya couldn't allow that.

She hung up and made her way downstairs. Marco would be waiting for her. There was a long drive ahead and she wanted to get to Lagoon City as soon as possible.

*

Maya sat in the car while Marco drove, watching Lagoon City come into view in the distance. She understood the reason for the name as soon as she saw it, picking up the shimmer of sunlight on the water of multiple lakes around it, making the city look as if it sat in the middle of some great lagoon. Skyscrapers and industrial buildings rose in a forest of steel and glass, while suburbs spread out in tendrils around the lakes, parks and greenery set in between them. There probably wasn't anywhere in the city that wasn't close to a lake.

She read through as much as she could find on the case while Marco sped them towards it all, going through the files that Samit had managed to supply, trying to make some sense of it.

She was staring at a picture of the victim attached to the file. Reba Andrews was a pretty, young Black woman with high cheekbones and large eyes that made her look even younger than the twenty-three she'd been when she died.

The next picture wasn't so pretty. It showed the crime scene, with her lying there abandoned on the stony edge of a lake, left casually, as if there wasn't any reason to try to rearrange her or move her now that she was dead. As if everything about her worth was just gone. It was disturbing to see, and not just because of the familiar horror that came with seeing a crime scene.

What was disturbing was just how similar this was to the work of the Moonlight Killer. He killed on the full moon. He strangled using a ligature. He abandoned his victims where they fell.

"What do you have?" Marco asked her as he drove, keeping his eyes on the road ahead.

"Reba Andrews was twenty-three when she was killed six months ago, on the night of the full moon. She was strangled with a ligature and left on the shore of one of the lakes here. The local police attributed it to the Moonlight Killer."

"And the FBI?" Marco asked. It was a good question. Just because the locals had decided that this had to be the Moonlight Killer, that didn't mean that Agent Swift's taskforce had to agree with it. In this case, though, they had. They'd looked at it closely, but hadn't been able to find anything.

"They thought the murder was consistent with his methods and timing. The details were pretty much identical, Marco. Not just the fact that Reba was killed with a ligature on the night of the full moon, but other things too."

Now, Marco briefly glanced across at her while he drove.

"Such as?"

Maya started to look through the files again

"The report from the scene suggests that Reba was left where she fell; that's a piece of the Moonlight Killer's MO that people have gotten wrong plenty of times before. There's also the fact that she's a young woman, his preferred victim type."

"But we know it can't be him," Marco pointed out. "That isn't the way this whole game of his works."

Maya nodded. "I know that. It's just… the pictures of her. She has that same delicate bone structure that all the women he kidnapped have, that same look, like there's something almost fragile about her, like she's on the verge of breaking."

It was probably a coincidence, but Maya couldn't help feeling that it might be more than that. There were too many similarities stacking up here.

"You sound almost as if you aren't convinced that it's a copycat," Marco said. He sounded surprised by that. "Do you think it might actually be him?"

Honestly, Maya didn't know *what* to think. On the one hand, the Moonlight Killer had consistently sent her to investigate cases that had been wrongly attributed to him, as if wanting to clear his reputation by casting aside any taint from the work of others. That seemed to make it obvious that this was someone else.

On the other hand, though, this case looked like such a perfect copy of his work that it was hard for Maya not to at least consider the possibility that it might be him.

"I don't know," Maya admitted. "It doesn't make sense that he would send us to look into his own work, but… what if that's his way of getting me to fail? What if he's sent me looking into one of his actual kills, given me a short deadline, and now he's hoping that I spend all that time going around chasing shadows until I fail?"

"What would he gain by doing that?" Marco asked in a reassuring tone. "You've said before plenty of times that he likes to stick to the rules of his game. He wouldn't cheat like that."

Maya hoped that it was true. She hoped that the Moonlight Killer wasn't setting her up to fail. The worst part was that, whether it was true or not, all she could do was proceed on the assumption that it was someone else and hope that she was able to find an answer in time.

"I hope you're right," Maya said. "But if it's not him, that begs the question of how someone has been copying him so precisely. Someone committed a murder that got all the details right, even the ones that normal people don't know about."

That made her worried again about the similarities, but also made her wonder if the copying might provide her with a way into this case.

Maybe if the killer had been looking for those details, he would have left a trail that she would be able to follow?

"Where do you want to start with all of this?" Marco asked.

"I have a message from Samit along with the files," Maya replied. "He's been in touch with local law enforcement like I asked. One of their detectives is going to meet us at the spot where the body was found when we get there."

"Reminds me of the way we met," Marco said with a smile.

It was almost exactly the same. As a result, Maya had found a partner who had helped her solve multiple murders, and who had somehow become far more to her in the process. They'd solved that case. Hopefully they would manage as much this time too.

Maya just hoped that the detective they met this time would be as helpful. If they were going to solve the case in time, they would need all the help they could get.

CHAPTER FIVE

Megan sat watchfully in the bunker that was her prison, trying to find anything else that might help her sister to locate her and the others being held there. She listened at the air vents, hoping that there would be something else distinctive there, the way there had been with the saw-whet owl's calls, then moved around the place in a steady circuit, checking every corner of it in case she'd missed something on the hundred passes before. It was as much about feeling that she was doing something as because she had any real hope of finding anything.

She knew that she looked ragged and worn as she did so. They all did down here: her, Melissa, Saoirse, Imogen, Lucy, and Adi. Six women, where once there had been twelve. Their captor gave them water to wash with and clean gray jumpsuits to wear, but that couldn't do enough to counteract the effects of weeks of fear and stress. Megan's dark hair was a tangled mess by now, and if her features had recovered from the bruises their captor had inflicted on her, they still had new lines of worry and dark rings under her eyes from a lack of good sleep in the cages he kept them in at night.

"I don't know why you're bothering with that," Saoirse said, as Megan continued her circuit. "You know there's nothing to find. *He* wouldn't leave anything like that. Even if he did, it would only be a trick."

Saoirse came from an Irish family, with red hair, pale skin, and deep green eyes. There was always a tough edge to her, maybe trying to offset the delicacy of her features. It was a delicacy, almost fragility, that she had in common with all the rest of them, impossible to ignore. Their captor had a type.

Megan had seen that almost at once when she'd been put in here. It was impossible not to, when stuck in this one space with the same group of women for so long. The only reasons she didn't try to get the information out to her sister was because she couldn't see how it would help Maya to save them all and because she suspected that it was something that her sister would already have noticed. Megan didn't want to risk sending out information with one of the women who got released if it wouldn't help.

But she couldn't be like Saoirse, either. She couldn't just give up the hope that things might work out at the end of this.

"I have to try to do something," Megan said. "Even if there's nothing to find, I have to at least make the effort."

"Why?" Saoirse demanded, clearly not understanding.

"Because I need that hope that things are going to be ok."

The other woman laughed then. "Of course they're not going to be ok. He's going to kill us all."

Megan shook her head. It was important not to give in to despair. "The others have been released. My sister wouldn't still be going along with his demands if they hadn't."

"Your sister," Saoirse said, with a note of anger. "I'm sick of hearing about your sister, Megan. Without her, we wouldn't be in this mess. If *he* didn't want to play some kind of game with her, then we never would have been kidnapped."

She kept on with an almost terrified inflection of respect every time she mentioned their captor. That worried Megan. It was bad enough that the man who held them had so much power over them without giving him more.

"Or maybe he would have just killed us instead," Megan said. She wasn't sure why she said it, except that she'd looked into their captor's eyes, and there had been something deadly there, something that wanted to kill. She had no doubt that was why the other woman was convinced that he was going to kill them, rather than letting them go. Everyone down here must know what kind of man he was by now.

"You're all right for now," Saoirse said, with a note of complaint, as if it wasn't fair that Megan didn't run the risk of being killed right away. "It's obvious that he'll keep you until last, but that doesn't mean you're safe, Megan. Sooner or later, it will be your turn, or your precious sister will break his rules one too many times."

"All the more reason to try to find something that will let her save us," Megan countered. She couldn't afford to get angry with the other woman, not when the confined space meant that they were forced together whether they liked it or not. She kept walking, away from Saoirse. There wasn't much space in the bunker that formed their prison, but Megan was going to give her as much as she could.

As she walked, she kept looking for any tiny identifying mark or unusual element that might help to locate this place. Anything she could pass on might be enough. It was hard not to give in to despair as she did so, though, because Megan really had walked this way a hundred times or more, not finding the answers she hoped for, but even the act of looking did something to help.

Had Tori, the last woman to be released, been able to give Maya the information that Megan had found last time, about the saw-whet owls? If so, it didn't seem as though it had been enough to lead her straight to this place. Not on its own. Megan hadn't expected that, though. It was a piece of information to help narrow things down. Maybe with enough of them, *then* Maya would be able to come rescue them.

Megan had to hope that was how this would end, because she wasn't sure how much longer any of them could stand being there. The other women she passed there looked restless now: Lucy was pacing back and forth in the central chamber, Melissa was doing calisthenics as if trying to burn off the boredom of being stuck there.

Megan knew the layout of this place perfectly now. There was a large central chamber, empty except for a big screen and a single chair in the middle, so that their captor could hold court like a king. There were the branching corridors, one of them holding the cages that he kept them in at night. There were a couple of old storerooms. There was the door that led up and out towards the outside world. Then there was the control room beyond a locked door, perfectly circular with a domed roof, where their captor kept his banks of screens and devices for surveillance, but also where he kept an empty circular space, a hook hanging over it to hold a captive by her hands. Just the thought of that space made Megan shudder with the memories of the violence he had inflicted on her there.

Was it possible that Maya would solve enough murders to see them all released and for this to be over? Her sister had been successful so far, but Megan had also seen how close she'd come to failing before. Their captor had enjoyed showing all of them Maya's difficulties with the cases, trying to prove that he was superior to her in every way. Sooner or later, he would arrange something that was impossible for her to solve in the time he set, and someone would die.

Megan didn't think that it would be her even then, but it was still a horrifying thought. He would keep her for last, but maybe that would be exactly when he chose to make it impossible to win his sick game. Maybe that was the final twist of all of this, with him releasing all the others only to try to hurt Maya as much as possible in the last act by killing her sister rather than sticking to the rules of his game.

Megan had to find a way to help her sister get to them before that.

She was still pacing the bunker when she heard the sound of the big door to the outside opening. That meant only one thing, their captor was coming to visit, perhaps to feed them.

He'd been inconsistent about that. There was no real sense of time down here beyond the times when he told them to go back to their cages and dimmed the lights in an artificial simulation of night. Even so, Megan was sure that he never fed them at a regular time, never came in to speak to them or intimidate them according to a schedule, only when he felt like it.

Apparently, he felt like it now.

He came in now, fully masked as always, so that there was no hint of his face other than those deep blue-gray eyes that seemed to have as much warmth in them as the ocean depths. Or possibly one of the predators that lived there. He was wearing all black, even down to his gloves, obviously determined to leave not even a hint of evidence that might link back to him. He was armed, as always, with a knife and a stun gun, more than enough to deter anyone from trying to break free even if he weren't also larger and more heavily built than any of them there.

He came in carrying a tray, setting down six bowls of chili. It was another means of control: the fact that he could dictate when they ate and slept, every detail of their lives.

"Bunnies!" he called out in that too jovial voice he sometimes adopted. "Oh bunnies! It's time for food. Come here!"

Megan went over, knowing that there was nothing to be gained by disobeying him in this place. She took one of the bowls of chili, eating with her hands since there was no cutlery.

"Since a couple of your number have tried to escape in their own ways, I have decided not to allow you anything that might be used as a weapon, however ineffectual," he said, obviously guessing Megan's frustration at that. His tone hardened slightly. "Besides, it helps to remind you all of your place. Every breath you take here, every moment you exist, is because I allow it. Everything here operates according to *my* rules."

Megan knew that as well as anyone. The problem was that, if they all kept playing by his rules, there was a good chance that some of them wouldn't survive. They had to find a way out of here.

The others came to get their food, grabbing bowls and moving as far away from their captor as they thought they could without him calling them out on it. Megan could see the fear on their faces every time he was close and that was only made worse by the fact that she felt exactly the same kind of fear, too.

The man who held them moved to his chair as the six of them ate, the mask obscuring his expression. Was there amusement there? Disdain? It was impossible to tell. Megan only knew that she hated him, regardless of what he thought of them then.

His eyes caught hers and she knew that he knew. He knew exactly what she thought about him and it didn't make any difference to him. All this business of them being his precious "bunnies" was simply for show, an affectation. Megan knew firsthand just how calculating and harsh he could be. He would kill them without hesitation or regret.

That icy look disappeared an instant later as he stood. "Good news, bunnies. I have set dear Maya another challenge, one that I'm sure we all hope she's up to. I would hate to have to kill one of you because she was too stupid to find an answer this time."

Megan could practically feel the fear around the room now.

"I have decided to be… democratic about it this time," he said. "Obviously, I need Megan alive, but the rest of you… well, you can decide among yourselves who it will be. Who dies if Maya fails? Who goes free if she succeeds? I will give you until tonight to decide."

"And if we can't decide?" Megan asked.

"Then I'll make you pick, Megan," he replied, in a voice far more charming than the words he spoke. "I'll make you pick, and if you refuse, I'll hurt them in front of you until you *do* pick. I know you've started to think of yourself as a bit of a leader among them, so I'll show you what that means."

He'd been watching, at least some of the time. That was hardly a surprise to Megan; she'd known he was watching almost from the moment she arrived here. But he couldn't watch all the time, and he hadn't done anything to show that he knew about the message she'd passed on through Tori.

His latest game didn't matter. They would pick someone. One of them would want to go home enough to risk it, especially when Maya had succeeded so many times before.

"Oh, one more thing," their captor said. "Before I go, I should tell you this part: Dear Maya has only three days this time. Three days, at midnight, or I'm sorry to say that it will be one of you who pays the price. Good luck choosing, bunnies."

CHAPTER SIX

Maya hadn't been sure what to expect from the lakeside where Reba Andrews had been found as she walked the short distance from the parking lot to the site. Obviously, after so long, it was no longer closed off as a crime scene, but a part of her had expected some remembrance of the crime to linger, for there to be a plaque or a something warning people to stay away from the spot where it had happened out of some kind of instinct.

Instead, the shore around the lake was busy and bustling, with plenty of people out there enjoying what was proving to be a pleasant, warm day. Maya might even have found it nice if it weren't for the reason why she was there. There were a few groups of kids running about, one group playing football, another playing music off to one side. Plenty of people seemed to be having picnics, while there were several small boats out on the lake and a couple of people fishing from the end of a small wharf. It made it hard to imagine that anyone had been killed there.

The lake itself was broad and kidney shaped, with trees around one side. The other was open to the city beyond. The water was largely flat, the sun gleaming off it like a mirror. Maya could see another lake in the distance, presumably with another beyond that, as part of the network of such lakes ringing the city.

Maya looked around, trying to find the spot that had been in the crime scene photographs, but it was hard to make out when the presence of so many people made everything seem so very different. The site of the murder could have been anywhere along the shore.

Then she spotted someone waving to her and Marco. It was a man in his late twenties, wearing a plaid jacket over dark slacks and a lighter shirt. He was around Maya's height, with dark hair and broad shoulders. Something about him screamed "cop" to Maya, after spending so long around local law enforcement. Given the way he was waving, it was just as obvious that he'd been able to pick them out as FBI too.

Maya made for him with Marco, meeting him in a spot a little way from the groups there to enjoy the lake.

"Agent Gray?" he said as he got close. "Detective Spinelli? I'm Detective Ben Keymer, of the Lagoon City PD's robbery homicide division."

He held out a hand for Maya to shake.

"Thank you for meeting us out here like this," Maya said. "I know you have other cases you need to work."

"If I can help to catch a serial killer, I'll do everything I can," he said. "My boss has told me to give you anything you need. It's just…"

He looked uncertain that he should say whatever was in his head.

"Just?" Maya asked.

"Do you actually think you're going to be able to do anything to catch the Moonlight Killer?"

Maya hoped so, she really did. He was the one who lay at the end of all this, possibly even behind this murder. Even if he wasn't, then ultimately Maya needed to find a way to catch him. She had to do that not just for her sister and the other women he had taken as his hostages, but also for all the others he might go on to kill if he was left out in the world. That wasn't what the detective meant, though, was it?

"We're going to do everything we can," Maya said. "But I have to warn you, a lot of the times with these cases, we find that it wasn't the Moonlight Killer."

All of the time so far, but until she had something more concrete, Maya didn't want to say it in this case. Not just because the detective would demand to know why she didn't think it was him, but also because of the strange similarities this case had to the Moonlight Killer's work. Maya wanted to be sure, one way or another, whether the Moonlight Killer was trying to fool her by including one of his own cases before she rejected it all out of hand.

Detective Keymer didn't seem put off by her saying that in the slightest. "You have to follow the evidence. But in this case, I'm pretty sure that the evidence points straight at the Moonlight Killer. It's just whether it gives you anything you can use to catch him."

"Why don't you walk us through the evidence?" Marco said, gesturing to the broad expanse of the shoreline. "Show us the spot where Reba Andrews was found and tell us what it was really like. You *were* there on the original investigation?"

"I was there. Me and my partner, although she's not on the force anymore."

That caught Maya's interest for a moment. "What happened?"

It was the kind of question it was probably better not to ask, but she couldn't stop herself. There were plenty of reasons someone might leave, but not all of them were good. Someone might just decide that the job wasn't for them, or move on to bigger and better things, but they might also be hurt or fired, shown to be corrupt in some way, or even killed in the course of their duties. Even if she'd just seen too much and ended up with the kind of PTSD that meant she couldn't keep going, it might be painful to mention. If it was any of those, then bringing up the possibility might not have been Maya's smartest move ever.

Instead, Detective Keymer lifted his hand, displaying a wedding ring with a smile that suggested he'd told this story a few times by now to different people.

"Life happened. We started off as partners and just gradually… drifted closer. We set a date, and only then found out that we were going to have a baby. After we were married, Lacy decided to stay home with the baby, because it didn't seem fair, risking both of us out chasing criminals."

"Congratulations," Maya said, because she couldn't think of anything else to say. She couldn't help thinking about herself and Marco in that moment, and the way they'd drifted closer to one another over the course of their investigations. Would they end up the way that Detective Keymer and his wife had? Would Maya find herself quitting the FBI because it felt too dangerous with a family?

That wasn't something Maya had ever thought about. It certainly didn't feel like something she wanted to do. She didn't want to give up her work. It also wasn't something that she had any time to consider right then, not when there was a killer out there somewhere in the city and they had only three days to catch him.

"Tell us about the scene," Maya said, trying to bring things back to the investigation.

"Of course. This way."

Detective Keymer led her and Marco down to a spot by the water's edge, not too far from a stack of boulders that looked as though they formed a natural wind break. They also potentially provided cover to anyone wanting to sneak up on someone. Was that the reason the killer had struck there?

"We think the killer waited for Reba Andrews in those rocks," Detective Keymer said. "Although it's also possible that he simply followed her. We know that she liked to walk along this beach in the evenings, so maybe the killer did too. She was found… here."

He gestured to a spot just a few feet from the water, seeming very certain about it. Maya tried to recall what she'd seen of the crime scene photographs, with Reba lying face down near the water, looking abandoned rather than posed.

"Who found the body?" Marco asked. That was a good question. Maybe it would point them at another potential suspect.

"A friend of the victim's," the detective replied. "She went out to meet her there at the shore, said she'd arranged to do it, and when she got there, she found the body. From what I understand, she screamed so loud that someone else along the shore called the police before they even realized what was happening."

Maya could only imagine how horrific it had to be for someone, finding one of their friends dead like that, but she wasn't sure it got them closer to finding their killer.

"What else can you tell us about the scene?" Maya asked the detective. The more details they got now, the more chance there was of getting an answer here.

"We ruled out a robbery early," Detective Keymer said. "Strangulation is unusual with that kind of thing anyway, but the killer also left behind a full wallet, the victim's phone, even some pearl or something of hers that was just lying there near the body. A thief would have taken *something*. After that, with it being the full moon, and with that method of killing… the FBI took over pretty quickly."

"Did that bother you?" Marco asked. He was obviously thinking about the way the case back in Cleveland had gone that he'd been the detective on, when the FBI had swooped in, insisting that it was the Moonlight Killer. On other cases, they'd run into cops who had actively tried to obstruct them, and who certainly hadn't liked them being there.

"Not so much," Detective Keymer said. "We have plenty of crimes of our own to look into without trying to add tracking down a serial killer to the list. We were happy for the assistance from the FBI."

That was one difference between him and Marco right there. When Maya had shown up in Cleveland, he'd made it clear that he wasn't happy with the way that the FBI's focus on the Moonlight Killer had stopped him from looking at any other possible leads. He'd wanted to be involved in all of it.

"What can you tell us about the victim?" Maya asked. "I guess you talked to her family and looked into her life."

"Until the FBI showed up, sure," Detective Keymer said. He took out an old fashioned notebook, obviously wanting to remind himself of the details. "Reba Andrews was twenty-three. She was just about to start a post-graduate course in organic chemistry, focusing on applications of graphene and related substances. There was a bunch of other stuff that I'm not even going to pretend I understand."

"So she was obviously clever," Maya said. "Did she have any boyfriends, girlfriends? Anyone who might have been a suspect in her personal life?"

"Her family said no," Detective Keymer said, "and we had no reason to doubt it based on her social media records. An ex-boyfriend."

"We'll need access to her social media," Maya said. If the detective couldn't get them in, she was pretty sure that Samit would be able to, but it seemed easiest just to ask.

"Of course, and if you need to borrow any office space, my boss has said that he'll find you something back at the department."

"That's very kind," Maya said, "but if I have enough dead time to be in an office on this one, I'm doing something wrong."

She didn't want to waste a single second while she was here.

Detective Keymer raised an eyebrow at that. "Are you in a hurry to solve this?"

Maya wondered how much to tell him. She didn't want to have to explain everything about the kidnappings to a local cop, didn't want to have to give away that information, even though that was exactly what she'd ended up doing with Marco. Thankfully, it was Marco who came to her rescue.

"We're in a hurry to solve *every* case," he said. "That's what our taskforce does. We go in and throw everything we have at a cold case over a few days to try to make some progress."

"And that works?" Detective Keymer asked, sounding skeptical about the concept. Maya could understand; it wasn't the way that cold cases usually worked.

Maya nodded. "More often than you'd think."

Detective Keymer shrugged. "Well, if you *do* need anything, all you have to do is call me. For now, I should get back to the department."

Maya let him walk off. In a lot of ways it was better to be able to look things over without that kind of outside interference. She wanted to be able to make her own judgements about the site of the murder, uninfluenced by the original investigation. She took her time looking around the scene, her old military instincts assessing it as an ambush spot. Of all the places on the beach, in the dark, this was probably the one that worked best.

“The killer picked this spot deliberately,” she said. “He might have been following her, but my guess is that he picked her out beforehand. This wasn’t random.”

“He picked this spot, but once he’d made the kill, he didn’t care enough to rearrange the body,” Marco pointed out. “That’s a lot of care over the killing, but none afterwards.”

Exactly the way the Moonlight Killer would have done it. That thought worried Maya even more. *Were* they dealing with one of his cases? Even knowing how unlikely it was, it was hard to be sure either way.

“Where do you want to go next?” Marco asked.

That was an important question. They only had a limited time here, so every decision Maya made mattered now. They couldn’t afford to waste time going in the wrong direction.

One possibility stood out from the others, one that might let her establish with greater certainty whether this was the work of the Moonlight Killer or not, but which might also give Maya some insight into any aspects of Reba’s life that might have led to her being targeted as a victim in some other way.

“I want to talk to Reba’s family.”

CHAPTER SEVEN

The Andrews' family home looked to Maya like exactly the kind of place where it would be good to bring up kids: not too far from the lake, with a sprawling yard and plenty of space for them to run around. It had obviously been cared for over the years, sitting in the midst of a quiet neighborhood of other, similar houses, the whole place having a homey feel to it.

There was a minivan on the driveway and even as Maya and Marco pulled up, a middle aged Black woman came out of the house with a trio of kids following close behind her. The youngest was probably around thirteen or fourteen, while the oldest was probably nearly twenty. She was clearly trying to organize them to get them to go into the minivan quietly, and just as clearly, that wasn't going to happen in any kind of orderly fashion.

Maya hurried forward, determined to catch up to them before they could leave. She didn't have enough time to wait and try to talk to them later.

"Ms. Andrews?" Maya said.

"Who wants to know?" There was a defensive note there that Maya guessed might have come from too many people coming around asking questions in the wake of her daughter's death. She probably thought that Maya was a reporter.

"I'm Agent Gray, with the FBI. This is Detective Spinelli." Maya fished out her ID for the other woman to look at. "You're Reba Andrews's mother?"

"I am," the other woman agreed. "Emma Andrews. You're here to talk to me about my daughter?"

Maya nodded. She caught the hint of trepidation there in the other woman's voice. It was a tone Maya had heard plenty of times before working cold cases. In a fresh case, the presence of law enforcement might be a comfort, but in a cold one, it was all too easy to view it as a disturbance, coming just as people had started to settle their lives back into some semblance of normality.

She knew from experience that she couldn't let that stop her. Especially not with so little time. Doing her work was the only way that this woman's daughter would finally get justice.

"Yes," she said. "I'm sorry, but we need to talk to you. We're re-investigating Reba's death, trying to find answers."

"What answers do you think you're going to find?" Emma asked. "It was that Moonlight Killer. Everyone said so. Are you telling me that you've found a way to catch him?"

Not yet. Maya had to bite back those words, because she couldn't afford to start explaining their significance to anyone who didn't need to know. She couldn't let the news get out that the man who had kidnapped her sister was the infamous serial killer, or her boss would want to know why Maya hadn't told him that weeks ago.

"We're working on it," Maya said, trying to keep her tone carefully neutral. "But we also think that it's important to investigate the case with fresh eyes, not making any assumptions about who might have done this."

"But it's *obviously* the Moonlight Killer," Emma said. She sounded as though she wanted that to be true. Maybe she did. Maybe even that unsatisfactory answer was still an answer of sorts, meaning that she and her family could move on.

Maya felt a little guilty as a result of disturbing the peace of this family, but it was what she had to do in order to catch a killer. In any case, there would be a far deeper, more complete kind of peace for them once she caught the real killer. If she could.

"We're still trying to establish whether that's the case," Marco said. "Can we talk to you about your daughter, Ms. Andrews?"

"Does it have to be now?"

"Please," Maya said. If she weren't working to such a short, lethal deadline, maybe she would have gone away and tried to come back after giving Reba's mother some more time to think about things, but she couldn't now, not with a woman's life hanging in the balance if she took too long over her investigation. There simply wasn't a moment to spare.

"All right. Tommy, look after everyone. I need to talk to these people for a minute."

She gestured to the house, then led Maya and Marco inside, obviously wanting to talk to them away from the children. The interior had that pleasant chaos that family homes sometimes got, with pictures everywhere of different children at recitals or sporting events, a small minefield of shoes abandoned in the hall, and a couple of tables that were covered in clutter that seemed to include everything from keys to sets of headphones, obviously left there so that everyone in the house could grab what they needed as they headed out.

Emma Andrews led the way through to a living room dominated by a couple of large gray couches. She gestured to one and Maya took a seat alongside Marco, close enough that the two of them could have touched. It took an effort from Maya *not* to touch him when he was that close, holding herself just slightly away from contact, having to remind herself that she was an FBI agent, there to do a job, and that her personal life had to stay separate from her professional life.

Emma took a seat opposite them on the other couch, leaning forward slightly as if she didn't really want to be there and was ready to leave at the first opportunity. Maya didn't blame her; she knew it couldn't be easy, talking about her murdered daughter like this. It wasn't something anyone wanted to have to do, but right then, Maya needed any information she could get.

"You really don't think that this is down to the Moonlight Killer?" Emma asked, getting out the first question.

"We're not sure yet," Maya replied, "but in the past, our taskforce has been called in on several cases where it looked like the Moonlight Killer's MO, only for it to turn out to be someone else."

It was the safest way to put it. If it weren't for the similarities to the Moonlight Killer's methods, Maya might have come out and said straight away that she didn't think it was him. Given everything that she'd seen so far, though, it was hard for Maya not to be a little more circumspect.

"So what does that mean?" Emma asked.

Marco answered. "It means that we need to look into every aspect of Reba's life to try to find out if there was any reason why someone might have wanted to kill her."

"Of course there wasn't!"

The suddenness and vehemence of that spoke volumes to Maya. There were times when it was easier for a family to believe that a serial killer might have done something, because that left their family member as a random victim, who hadn't been caught up in anything that might lead to their death. Emma Andrews was assuming that the only way her daughter might be killed if it wasn't down to a well-known serial killer was if she'd done something wrong, something to deserve it. The world didn't work like that, though. Being a good person didn't make anyone safe.

"We're not saying that Reba was involved in anything she shouldn't have been," Maya said. She watched carefully for any reaction from the mother to suggest excessive relief at that, which in turn might suggest that Reba *had* been caught up in something illegal.

No, nothing, there was no sign that her mother knew something that she and Marco needed to. "We just want to know more about her life. What was she like?"

The question seemed to take away a little of Emma's defensiveness. Maya had been hoping for that, trying to pull her back into memories of her daughter. Those, in turn, might lead them to the kind of information they needed.

"Reba was always such a good girl. So clever. She did so well at college, and then to be taken on as a grad student like that… we were so proud of her."

"She was about to start studying in chemistry?" Maya asked. That was what it had said in the file.

Emma nodded. "I didn't understand all the details of it, but it was a big new chance for her. She'd been on the verge of just going to get a job with her degree, but the offer came through, and she said she had to accept it. She said she wanted to work on the most important technologies, and that her work might make a real difference."

"So she was changing direction?" Maya said. Changing direction, on the cusp of transforming. All the things that the Moonlight Killer liked.

"That's right."

Maya fell silent as she processed that. Reba Andrews had been on the verge of a big change in her life, just like all the women on Maya's evidence board back home. Just like so many of the Moonlight Killer's victims. It was something that hadn't made it into the press, something that Maya had only recently worked out.

Could it be a coincidence? Had someone else picked Reba out as a victim, not knowing about this huge change in her life? Or had someone worked out what Maya had worked out about the Moonlight Killer and adapted his methods to fit?

That second option seemed unlikely, when the only reason Maya had been able to do it was with the group of kidnap victims to work from. She'd worked out who the kidnapper was and she'd worked out what his kidnapping victims had in common. Someone who didn't have that information wouldn't be able to see through the noise of fake Moonlight Killer cases to pick out the underlying pattern.

So was this a Moonlight Killer case after all? That was a terrifying prospect.

"Did your daughter often go down to the lake at night?" Marco asked. Maya hadn't realized how long she'd been silently lost in her thoughts until he asked it.

"Are you going to say it's her fault she was killed because she was out alone?" Emma demanded.

"No, of course not," Maya said.

"The press did. They insinuated all kinds of things about my Reba. Said she had no business being out at night, like it isn't a free country. They made it sound like she was asking to be killed."

"I'm just trying to establish how easy it would have been for someone to find out that Reba went there," Marco said. "If she went there a lot, then someone who knew her might have been able to find out about it, maybe even someone who didn't know her, if she talked about it online. If it's something she only did that one time, though, then maybe that's significant."

Because in that case, there was a chance that she'd arranged to meet someone there, and that someone had been the one to kill her. For Maya, the answer to this question potentially took the case in very different directions.

"Reba used to go up there all the time, ever since she was a little girl," Emma said. "She'd stay out as late as I let her, because she liked to look at the stars. When she got older, she used to know all their names. She said it was a reminder of just how big the universe is, but also just how much we could know if we tried."

So it was normal for her and anyone who knew her might have been able to find it out. That didn't narrow down the pool of suspects the way Maya would have liked.

"She was starting to stay out later, too," Emma said. "She said it was for her new studies, because for a lot of the labs she would have to run things overnight. Reba always was a bit of a night owl."

That was interesting, but Maya wasn't sure if it got them any close to finding Reba's killer.

"Did she have a boyfriend at the time of her death?" Marco asked.

Emma shook her head. "Not then, no."

"But before?" Maya asked, picking up on it.

"She'd broken up with her boyfriend, Oli, maybe a week before. But the police talked to him, I think."

Maya nodded. She still wanted to talk to him again though, just to make sure that the local police had been thorough in their investigation. She wasn't sure if there were even details of his alibi in the file.

"Can you think of anyone else, anyone at all, who might have wanted to hurt your daughter?" Maya asked. "Had anyone argued with her about anything recently before her death, no matter how small?"

Emma shook her head, though. "No, I'm sorry. Look, I've told you everything I know, and I have to get moving or the kids are going to cause chaos out in the minivan."

Maya nodded, understanding. This woman didn't want to keep getting dragged back into the details of her daughter's death. "Thank you for your time, Ms. Andrews."

"Personally, I think you're *wasting* your time," Emma replied. "This was that serial killer, the Moonlight Killer. There's no other explanation that makes sense. If you can find him, great, but if not, why tear up the past like this?"

Maya could hear the pain there. She knew the hurt that a cold case investigation could cause, reopening old wounds that had just started to heal. Worse, there was a part of her that was starting to agree with Reba's mother about this being the work of the Moonlight Killer.

Maya couldn't just leave it at that, though. She had to investigate every possibility when it came to Reba's death, starting with the people who had been closest to her.

CHAPTER EIGHT

Maya started by checking on Reba's ex-boyfriend, Oli. A quick glance at the police records gave her a full name for him, Oli Brant, and an address in Lagoon City. He seemed to have been discounted from the original investigation quickly, but Maya couldn't tell if that was because there was actually a reason to, or because Detective Keymer and the others here had simply assumed that this was the work of the Moonlight Killer. There weren't any details of an alibi set down. Maya would have to ask Keymer about that.

As she and Marco drove over to the address, he seemed a little quiet.

"Are you ok?" Maya asked him.

"Yes, I'm just thinking about the similarities between all of this and the time we first met."

Maya had been thinking about some of those similarities too. There had been a body by a lake back in Cleveland as well, and there too, she hadn't been sure whether it was the Moonlight Killer or not. This situation was uncomfortably similar.

"Just think," Maya said. "Without all of this, we might never have met."

Marco cocked his head to one side. "It feels wrong to say that I'm grateful for a serial killer making us both jump through hoops for his amusement, but I'm still glad I got to meet you."

"Me too," Maya assured him, although she *definitely* wished that it had been under other circumstances. Ones that didn't place her sister in danger. On the other hand, though, without this situation, Marco would presumably have never been forced to leave his job as a cop in Cleveland, and the two of them certainly wouldn't be working so close together. There wouldn't have been a chance for them to grow quite as close as they had. Maya was grateful that had happened, even as she hated the rest of it.

"I think we're here," Marco said, pulling up in front of a small apartment block.

"Time to see what Oli Brant knows, and if he has any involvement in all of this," Maya said.

She led the way to the apartment block, hitting the intercom beside the name Brant.

"Yeah?" a voice said through the intercom. It was male and young, which suggested that they'd probably found the person they wanted to speak to.

"Oli Brant? I'm Agent Gray, with the FBI. My partner and I would like to speak to you in connection with the death of Reba Andrews."

Maya tried to keep her tone formal, making it all sound as official as possible. It seemed to work, because Maya could hear the nervousness in Oli Brant's voice as he answered.

"I guess you'd better come inside."

He buzzed them through. Maya and Marco made their way up to his apartment, where he was waiting for them at the door, with it only half open. It seemed obvious that he didn't want to let them any further inside than that. Maya found herself wondering if he was worried about them spotting something inside the apartment and her nose gave her the answer in the form of the faint scent of weed coming from somewhere behind Oli.

Oli was a tall, skinny young man in his early twenties, with ginger hair and a moustache that didn't really suit him. He was good looking in a gawky kind of way, but he looked pretty nervous to see Maya and Marco there suddenly and it seemed obvious the moment they walked up that he wanted to get rid of them as quickly as possible.

"Why do you want to talk to me?" he demanded.

"Because you and Reba Andrews broke up not long before she was murdered," Maya replied. "I'd like some more detail about what happened and why."

"That was a year ago," Oli answered. "How am I meant to remember all the details?"

Maya didn't buy that for a moment. Nor, it seemed, did Marco.

"Your ex-girlfriend died. My guess is that you remember every detail of the days leading up to her death, because you've been over them a million times in your head, trying to make sense of everything."

Oli looked, if anything, more defensive then. "So what if I have? I haven't done anything wrong, and I don't have to answer any of your questions."

Maya nodded. "You don't, but *if* you don't, then I have to start wondering what you're hiding, Oli. For a start, why are you keeping that door so carefully closed? Is it because you know we'll spot your drugs if we open it?"

Oli shook his head quickly, but the smell coming from his apartment belied his denial.

"I don't know what you're talking about."

"You do," Maya countered, "and if you don't start answering some of our questions, I'm going to claim probable cause and push that door open."

She saw Oli swallow. She'd been hoping for this to be friendlier, but he was refusing to talk to them and they needed to establish exactly what his role in all of this was.

"What do you want to know?" Oli demanded.

Maya thought for a few moments. "What exactly happened between you and Reba?"

"She… she caught me messaging this other girl. Nothing serious, but she just blew it all up out of proportion. She broke up with me, wouldn't even listen to me when I tried to explain it all to her."

"Did you know how much she liked to go down to the lake?" Marco asked. It seemed like a sudden change of direction, but Maya understood what he was doing. They'd just established that Oli had a potential motive, so now Marco was trying to work out if Oli knew enough about his ex's habits to have had an opportunity to kill her.

Oli gave a kind of one shouldered shrug, still not relinquishing his grip on the door. "Everyone who knew her knew that. I'd go walking there with her sometimes. She liked to look at the stars."

"Where were you the night she died, Oli?" Maya asked.

"You think it was me? You think *I* did that to her? The cops already cleared me!"

"If that's the case, you won't mind telling us where you were," Maya said. She wasn't going to let it go that easily. If Oli had a solid alibi, that was fine, but she needed to know either way.

"I was out at a bar with another girl," Oli said, sounding faintly embarrassed by it. "Ok? The police checked it all at the time. Witnesses, security footage, all of it."

Maya wasn't just about to take his word for it though, so she got out her phone and called Detective Keymer.

"Detective, this is Agent Gray, from earlier."

"Hello, Agent, did you need something?"

"I'm talking to Oli Brant. He tells me that your department checked his alibi out thoroughly at the time of the murder and he was cleared. Is that correct?"

There was a brief pause on the other end of the line. "The ex-boyfriend? Yes. We found plenty of security footage to show he couldn't have been there at the time Reba Andrews was murdered. Plus the girl he was with was willing to corroborate that he went home with her."

Without the footage, that might not have meant much, but with it, it meant that there was no way that Oli could have been there that night to kill Reba. He wasn't the killer they were looking for. If more details had been in the file, there might not even have been a reason to come here.

"Thank you, Detective," Maya said and hung up. She looked over to Oli. "It looks like your story checks out. But you could still help us, Oli."

"Help you? After you pretty much accuse me of murdering my ex?"

"We didn't accuse you of anything," Maya said, "but we *did* have to check your alibi to be able to eliminate you as a potential suspect."

"Or you could just have accepted that the cops ruled me out a year ago," Oli shot back. He sounded agitated now. He obviously didn't want to speak to them. "You want to know who you should check out? Try that crazy friend of hers, Ceris, the one who found her. From what I hear, the police never even looked twice at her. Didn't care that she'd had a crush on Reba for as long as I can remember."

He'd obviously had enough of answering questions, and simply shut the door, blocking Maya and Marco out. Marco went to knock on the door, but Maya caught his arm.

"He's not going to give us anything else," Maya said. "He's too hostile. Besides, he may already have given us something useful."

She put in another call to Detective Keymer.

"Two calls in just a few minutes," the detective said. "I guess I should feel honored."

"I just wanted to know what you remember about the young woman who found the body," Maya said. "She was a friend of Reba's. Ceris something?"

"Ceris O'Dell," Detective Keymer supplied. "I remember her being pretty distraught when she found the body. Completely hysterical. We couldn't even question her properly, she was so upset by it. Any mention of it would just start her crying again. After a while, it just seemed cruel, when it seemed so obvious that the Moonlight Killer was involved."

"Was she ever considered as a potential suspect?" Maya asked.

She heard Detective Keymer laugh, briefly. "If you'd seen the state of her when we showed up, you wouldn't ask that. She was so distraught there's no way she could have planned and executed something so cold-blooded."

"Oli Brant seems to think she had a crush on her friend," Maya said. "If that wasn't reciprocated, then maybe there's the beginning of a motive there."

"That's a bit thin, Agent Gray, but if you really want to talk to her, I guess I can look up an address for her." There was a pause and the sound of typing at the other end of the line. "Turns out that there's another reason we didn't follow up with her: about a month after the murder, she moved away from Lagoon City. Something about going to stay with her grandmother."

Instantly, Maya was more suspicious than she had been. Reba's friend had moved away that soon after the murder? It was hard not to read that as someone trying to get as far away from the scene of the crime as possible. As for the rest of it, just being distraught at the death wasn't the same thing as proof that she wasn't involved. She might have been distressed at what she'd just done, or even acting to fool the police into discounting her as a potential suspect.

"Thank you, Detective Keymer. Could you find out where she went?"

"I guess the DMV will have details for her grandmother." More sounds of typing came in the background. "Ah, here we are. It's an address in Harrisburg. I'll send it to your phone."

Harrisburg was back the way they'd come, and most of an hour's drive away. That raised a difficult question for Maya: given how little time she had to solve this case, was it worth it to go out there to speak to one young woman?

Maya knew the answer as soon as she asked the question. This was someone the police had discounted as a potential suspect almost straight away, someone who had never been looked into or even really questioned, despite being the first person there at the scene. Someone who had moved away as soon as they thought they could after the murder. All of that felt suspicious.

At the very least, Ceris O'Dell was an important witness who might be able to tell them more about what she'd seen when she found her friend dead. She could also prove to be the killer, and if Maya let this go because the drive wasn't convenient in her timeframe, then she could be throwing away the best chance of solving this case.

She and Marco had to go to Harrisburg.

CHAPTER NINE

Marco wasn't quite sure what to make of their sudden journey to Harrisburg. He understood the reasoning behind Ceris O'Dell being a potential suspect, but he could also see Maya growing less sure as they made their way there.

He knew why because he knew Maya. The thing that would worry her most right now was the time involved, the threat of the looming deadline. An hour wasn't a long drive, but when it would be the same going back and when they didn't even know if they were going to get anything out of this journey, it probably felt like an eternity to Maya.

Marco had seen the pressure of these cases drive Maya to the edge before, working until she dropped in an effort to make more time to solve the murders. He just had to hope that it wouldn't be like that here. He cared too much about Maya to watch her go through all that yet again.

"We're doing the right thing," Marco said as they pulled up outside a small suburban home in a slight state of disrepair, with a cheap, dented Ford parked outside. "Coming here, it's something we need to do."

"I'm just thinking of all the other things we could do with this time," Maya said. A part of her wondered if the two of them should split up, but for the moment, she wanted her partner with her for this.

Marco nodded. He'd known that was what it would be.

"We can't just ignore this friend who found Reba's body, though," he said. "Especially not after what Oli Brant said about her having a crush on Reba. That gives us a potential motive if Reba rejected her, and finding the body… well, that explains away any physical evidence."

He saw Maya nod.

"I've been reading the reports on the evidence. There was DNA evidence from Ceris on Reba's body that the coroner put down to an attempt at CPR, and to pulling away the ligature."

"That could be true," Marco said, "or it could be because she killed her friend and then faked everything afterwards. Either way, we have to know."

They could get this done and still get back to Lagoon City in plenty of time to keep working other angles in the case if this one didn't pan out. If it did, they would have finished their investigation, well ahead of the deadline the Moonlight Killer had set.

Marco wasn't sure how he felt being the only other one who knew exactly who the kidnapper behind the postcards was. On one level, he was simply grateful that Maya trusted him enough to let him in on that secret. On another, he was worried about what might happen to her when the news of it finally got out. Maya might be the head of her own taskforce now, but Marco still wasn't sure if that would be enough to shield her from the fallout.

Marco just had to hope, and to be there for her whatever happened.

"You're right," Maya said. "Let's get in there. This whole thing with her has me suspicious. I want to know what's going on here."

Marco could hear a very familiar note of hope there as the two of them got out of the car and headed for the door to the property. He'd seen that excitement in her before as she'd gotten hold of a clue. There was a tenacity to her then that was always impressive to watch, running down leads until she finally got to the truth. It was just one of the traits Marco liked so much about Maya.

The door opened as they approached, revealing a woman who was probably in her sixties, whose red hair was fading to white in places and who stood a little shorter than Maya, which made her probably a head shorter than Marco was. She was wearing a floral print skirt and a white blouse, with a yellow cardigan over the top and a string of pearls around her neck.

"Whatever you're selling, we're not interested," she said.

Marco saw Maya pull out her badge. "We're with the FBI, ma'am. We're looking for Ceris O'Dell."

"Then we're *definitely* not interested."

Marco and Maya were almost up to the older woman now.

"We need to talk to Ceris," Maya said. "It's about-"

"Do you think I don't *know* what it's about? The FBI here? There's only going to be one thing that all of this is about. You want to talk about the girl who died, Reba Andrews."

"We do," Marco said, stepping in. Maya was good at drawing connections, but her need to find answers to save her sister could sometimes make her hard-edged and unsympathetic. "We're just trying to find answers, for Reba's family, and to stop the person who did this from killing again."

"And what about *my* family?" the woman said. "What about my granddaughter and the way it's going to affect her, with you being here?" She shook her head. "No, I'm not going to let you talk to her."

Marco could see the tension in Maya's face as Ceris's grandmother said that. He could tell how suspicious she was now, simply because of the denial. They had a potential suspect and her grandmother wasn't even letting them talk to her? Marco knew just from looking that Maya was starting to assume that this was just another way for Ceris O'Dell to avoid scrutiny, a way for her to try to get away with murder. Even Marco found his suspicions rising a little. This might just be a grandmother being overprotective, but what if it was more than that?

"I have to insist," Maya said. She still had her badge out. "If your granddaughter won't talk to us willingly, then maybe she'd prefer it if we did this at an FBI field office or a local police station."

The threat took Marco a little aback. With some local scumbag who was trying to be difficult, maybe, but with a random woman whose grandmother was trying to protect her? The lack of time on all of this was starting to show, making Maya impatient. Marco understood that she was doing everything she could to protect her sister, but he still suspected that there were more diplomatic ways to do it.

Marco did his best to smooth things over.

"Maybe it's better if we just talk to Ceris," he said. "We can sort all of this out, and no one has to be upset."

The grandmother still looked doubtful, but when she looked over at Maya and her set expression, she nodded. She obviously realized that she didn't have a lot of choice in the matter. It was clear that Maya wasn't going to back down on this. That she really *might* insist on doing this down at a local police department if there was no other choice. Ordinarily, Marco admired her determination, but sometimes it could spill over into something harder-edged, something without any give in it, pushed there by the threat that the Moonlight Killer posed to the lives of his captives.

The grandmother stepped back, away from the door to let them both pass.

"Just… promise me that you'll be careful with her. She… she's been through a lot."

"We'll be as tactful as we can," Marco promised. He looked over to Maya as he said it, hoping that it was true. It was hard to tell what she would do sometimes, when she thought that she was on the way to answers and there was only a limited time in which to get them. Marco could understand that, though. He couldn't imagine what he would be like if it were *his* family in danger.

They went inside with Ceris's grandmother, into a house that had been painted in quiet, calm pastel shades, with the drapes partly drawn to keep out too much harsh light, as if the whole place had been designed to be as peaceful as possible. They went through into a lounge, with large all enfolding armchairs that seemed like they'd been there for decades.

There was a woman curled up on one of those armchairs, young, blonde-haired, and almost painfully thin. She was wearing a gray cable knit sweater and leggings, with bare feet, her knees drawn up to her chest as if to protect herself from the world. Her head snapped around to look at them as they came in, revealing wide blue eyes, slightly red-rimmed from crying. There was fear there in her expression, but also more pain than Marco could have imagined.

Marco could see almost instantly that this wasn't some psychopath who could plan a murder in detail, make it look just like the Moonlight Killer's work, and then only pretend to be distraught afterwards. This wasn't acting. This was real pain, the pain of seeing her friend killed.

Marco gave Maya a warning look, but it wasn't necessary. It seemed that she'd seen exactly what Marco had. She still approached Ceris, moving to sit in a chair next to her, but she was moving slower now, much more carefully and quietly, obviously trying not to disturb her.

"Ceris," she said. "I'm Maya. I'm an agent with the FBI. Would it be all right to talk to you a little?"

When Ceris spoke, her voice was shaky. "This… this is about Reba. About that night."

Marco saw Maya nod. "We're just trying to get more of a picture of what happened then. Do you think you could tell us about that night?"

"I…"

Marco saw the young woman's breathing speed up. Her grandmother was there by her side almost instantly.

"Remember what they taught you at Aspens, Ceris. Go through your routines."

Ceris was taking deeper, slower breaths now, obviously working hard to try to calm herself. Her eyes were shut tightly and it was several seconds before she opened them again.

"I… I don't think I can talk about finding her," Ceris said. She sounded both apologetic and afraid.

"I understand," Maya replied. "Can I ask what Aspens is?"

"It's... a psychiatric facility," Ceris replied. She winced at the words. "I spent some time there when things got too bad after... what happened. They said I have PTSD. It's why I moved here with my grandmother."

The more Marco heard, the more he was convinced that this young woman wasn't a killer. Yes, it was possible that guilt had done this to her, but this didn't look like guilt, just the effects of seeing something no one should have to. He'd seen victims before and those around them. He'd seen the effects that the worst kind of violence could have on them.

"Can I ask you a couple of questions about things *before* you found Reba?" Maya asked.

Ceris nodded, although even then, she didn't look very certain to Marco.

"Did you arrange to meet her down at the lake?"

That got another slightly shaky nod.

"And where were you before you went there?"

"At... at the local library. There was a book group."

That was something that would be easy to check.

"If I'd just gotten there faster..." Ceris began.

Marco saw Maya put a hand on her shoulder. "There's nothing you could have done. The coroner's report suggests that Reba was killed an hour before you got there."

Which was also why the book group was important. It meant that Ceris had an alibi and this wasn't someone breaking down because she'd killed, but because of what she'd seen. It meant that they were making things worse for her just by being there.

"Were there any parts of Reba's life that she didn't tell other people about?" Maya asked. "She was your closest friend, right? Did she have any secrets that she shared with you that she didn't tell anyone else?"

"She used to tell me about guys and things," Ceris said. "But there wasn't anything she told me right before... I'm sorry, this is too much. I can't..."

Her grandmother was there then, moving between Maya and Ceris, her expression determined in spite of the authority of the FBI. "That's enough. My granddaughter isn't up to this. You need to leave."

Maya started to stand, but Marco saw her suddenly stop, staring at Ceris's grandmother. It took him a second or two to realize that she was staring at the string of pearls around the older woman's neck. Something had obviously clicked into place for her, but what? What could pearls possibly mean?

"Ceris, just one more question and we'll go," Maya said. "Did Reba own any jewelry? Specifically, did she have any pearls or opals, anything like that?"

Marco felt sure that Ceris wasn't going to answer, particularly not with her grandmother trying to usher the two of them out of there as quickly as possible. When she did speak, it was in a small voice, barely audible.

"No, nothing like that."

"Thank you, Ceris, you've helped us a lot," Maya said.

Marco went with her as the grandmother showed them out in a way that made it clear they were no longer welcome there. He had to wait until they were outside before he asked the obvious question.

"What was that about pearls?" He didn't get it.

"Detective Keymer said that it didn't look like a robbery, because they even left her pearl by the body," Maya said. "It didn't mean anything to me at the time, but it seemed odd, there being just a single pearl. And if Reba didn't own anything like that…"

Now he understood, so Marco finished it for her. "Where did it come from?"

He saw Maya nod. "We need to get back to Lagoon City. I want to see this pearl for myself."

CHAPTER TEN

Maya had made sure that Detective Keymer was waiting for her and Marco when they pulled up in front of Lagoon City's main police precinct. He was standing out front, looking slightly surprised at the speed with which Maya ran out of the car almost as soon as it drew to a halt, heading for the precinct.

"Do you have what I asked about here?" Maya asked as she came up to him. She could imagine far too many situations in which Reba Andrews's effects would have been passed back to her family, making it impossible to check.

To her relief, though, Detective Keymer nodded. "Everything's set up. The item is waiting in the evidence room, along with the jeweler you requested. Do you want to tell me what this is about, Agent Gray?"

"I'll explain once we get in there," Maya said. She wanted to be sure about all of this before she said too much.

Marco had caught up now. He was looking a little tired because he'd been the one doing all the driving. It was a reminder of just how much easier his presence could make these cases for Maya. Without him, she wouldn't have solved anywhere near as many cases as she had. She might even have lost her sister by failing to solve one of these cases.

She hoped that this time, his help in getting her to Harrisburg and back would pay off, letting her find the killer.

"I take it that you got something out of talking to Ceris O'Dell?" Detective Keymer asked as he led the way into the building. "Since you haven't arrested her, I take it she wasn't involved?"

"She's just an unfortunate young woman suffering from PTSD because of what she saw," Marco supplied. "We checked her movements on the way back and she couldn't have gotten to the beach earlier than she said. She *did* tell us one important thing, though."

Maya saw the detective tilt his head inquisitively. "And what was that?"

"That Reba didn't own anything similar to the piece of jewelry found with the body," Maya said. "Which means that it was placed there, potentially by the killer."

Now, Detective Keymer looked interested. He seemed to understand the urgency of what Maya was trying to do, keeping pace with her as she hurried into the building. He led the way through into a police precinct where the ground floor had the usual sense of chaos that came with serving a vibrant community. There were officers coming and going, a couple dragging in a man they'd arrested, ready to be processed, people waiting in a small area at the front of the precinct, hoping that someone could see them about a crime or there to give evidence.

It was the kind of place that reminded Maya of the differences between day-to-day police work and working as a cold cases agent for the FBI. Maya didn't have to deal with small local crimes, picking up an ever changing caseload. Instead, she had exactly one thing to worry about in her job: catching those who had committed crimes previously attributed to the Moonlight Killer, in an effort to free the women he had kidnapped. Of course, the price she paid for that was the game and its terrible stakes that he'd forced her into. She had to succeed or women would die.

For now, that meant following Detective Keymer through the precinct, then down a flight of stairs to a basement. There was an evidence room there, set behind a solid door, locked with a keypad. Inside, Maya found a middle aged man there wearing a tweed suit and glasses. He was sitting at a table waiting for the three of them, a selection of jeweler's tools set out in front of him.

"Agent Gray," Detective Keymer said. "This is Mark Vincent, the jeweler you requested."

"It's a pleasure to meet you, Mr. Vincent," Maya said, holding out a hand for him to shake, but her attention was on the table.

A single gemstone sat there on a black velvet cloth that the jeweler had obviously brought with him, shining with a silvery opalescence, polished to a high sheen.

"Is that the 'pearl' that was found on Reba Andrews's body?" Maya asked.

Detective Keymer nodded. "That's the one. I signed it out of evidence myself and Mr. Vincent has been examining it for half an hour now."

Maya looked over to the jeweler. "What can you tell us about it, Mr. Vincent?"

"Well, I'm not sure how much detail you want…"

"Anything you can tell us could prove useful," Maya said. She was aware of Marco nearby, looking down at the stone as if it would give up the killer if he only looked at it for long enough. Maya found herself hoping the same.

"Well, let's start with the basics," the jeweler said. "This is *not* a pearl, but what is commonly termed a moonstone, that is to say that it is a variety of orthoclase, in this case shaped to resemble a pearl. Stones like this are not particularly valuable, since it has a number of inclusions that make it less pure in its color. The most valuable are clear blue types, but those are largely mined out in Myanmar, where they're found, so new stones of that quality are relatively rare. Indeed, they have been all but mined out these days. Lesser stones like this are more common. I would guess that this has been worked recently, tumbled to create the sheen you see."

Maya took that in, but she latched onto one word more than the others. One word that seemed incredibly significant in the context of the case, impossible to ignore. "Did you say *moonstone*?"

"Yes," the jeweler said, "that's right."

A moonstone under the moon. That *had* to be significant.

"Where would someone get something like that?" Marco asked.

"Possibly from a jeweler," Mr. Vincent replied, "but in this case, where the stone has been recently tumbled but not set in a pendant or cabochon, I would guess that someone has processed this from raw moonstone."

"Can you write up a report for us on everything there is to know about this particular stone?" Maya said. "I want every detail I can get on it. Especially if any of those details might make it possible to trace it."

If they could trace the stone, then they might be able to follow it all the way back to the killer. She gestured for Marco and Detective Keymer to step outside with her.

"Is that it?" Detective Keymer asked, obviously wondering why he'd gone to the trouble of getting in a jeweler for so little.

Maya waited until they were outside the evidence room before she explained what it meant.

"It's a moonstone, placed on Reba Andrews's body when she was murdered on the night of the full moon."

"Yes," Detective Keymer said. "I got that part. What does it prove?"

Marco stepped in. "For one thing, it proves that this wasn't anything to do with the Moonlight Killer. He's never left this kind of calling card at the site of one of his kills, and there's no reason to think the moonstone belonged to the victim."

Maya nodded. That was one of the main things that the presence of the stone showed, and she felt a sudden, almost overwhelming wave of relief that it *did* show that. She'd been worried that the Moonlight Killer had been playing a sicker game than usual with her by sending her to look at one of his own kills, but now she knew that this was just someone with a similar MO.

The moonstone showed more than that, though.

"It also tells us a lot about what we're dealing with," Maya said. "Leaving it there has to be part of the killer's MO, and that suggests that even if this isn't the Moonlight Killer, we're not just dealing with an angry ex-boyfriend or a friend who wanted more. It also suggests that this wasn't random. At the very least, the killer planned to kill in that time and place, and since Reba was alone in an otherwise lonely spot, that suggests that she was targeted."

Maya gave that a second or two to sink in with Detective Keymer.

"Are you saying we have a serial killer who isn't the Moonlight Killer? A home grown serial killer?"

"I don't know yet," Maya said. "A serial killer implies multiple murders. If we're very lucky, this was a one off murder with a strange MO that means something to the killer."

She said lucky, but from the point of view of the case that would make things more difficult. There wasn't any physical evidence to go on other than the moonstone, so other murders might help to provide a pattern that Maya could work with, following it back to the killer. As horrible as it was to think it, she found herself hoping for other murders that fit the pattern.

"But you don't think it's likely," Detective Keymer said. His tone suggested that he didn't either.

Maya shook her head. "It's too neat."

"Meaning?"

Again, Marco answered that one, obviously understanding far more about it than the local detective.

"You've seen murders before where it's the first time someone has killed," he said. "When I worked robbery/homicide in Cleveland, I saw my share of them. They were mostly sloppy. People lashing out at random. People too angry to think straight about any of it. Even the ones who planned got things wrong. Someone like this who is striking without a trace… either he planned this for a long time, obsessed about it, or he's killed before."

Maya saw detective Keymer pale slightly at the thought of a home grown serial killer in his town. Maya didn't blame him for that in the slightest. At least the Moonlight Killer moved from place to place, striking and moving on so that there wouldn't be any need to worry about more murders in the near future. With a serial killer resident in the area, though, they wouldn't stop until Maya and Marco found them and *made* them stop. The young women of Lagoon City wouldn't be safe until then.

"So, how do we find this killer?" Detective Keymer asked.

Maya had been thinking about that question for much of the drive back to the city. "The first thing we need to do is find out if there are any other victims. Can you search through case files in any local murders?"

"If we go back to my workstation, sure."

They headed upstairs, going to the second floor, where Detective Keymer's workstation was as pristine as if he'd only just been assigned it. There were a couple of personal photographs of what Maya assumed were his former partner and now wife, but other than that it was pretty much empty. He was obviously too busy trying to catch bad guys for more than that.

Detective Keymer logged into the system and sat there in front of his computer, looking up at Maya.

"Ok, so what are we looking for?"

"This is an active killer," Maya said, "So let's only search for the last couple of years for now."

A part of that was because the Moonlight Killer had mostly sent her after murderers who were still active, potentially about to kill more people. Maya doubted that had anything to do with a desire to protect the wider public from such monsters. More likely, he wanted to make sure that more crimes wouldn't be wrongly attributed to him. He was proud of his work and only wanted *his* crimes to be recognized as his.

"So, we have all murders from two years as a starting point," Detective Keymer said. It was a smaller number than it would have been in a bigger city, but Maya could still see that it was too many to go through by hand in any reasonable time. Not when they had such immense time pressure.

"Restrict it to any with strangulation as the method of killing," Marco suggested. "Specifically with a ligature, rather than with bare hands."

That cut down the list a lot, but there would still be plenty of cases that weren't relevant. This was where Maya hoped the moonstone would help to narrow things down further.

“Can you word search in the files now?” she asked. “Search for ‘moonstone,’ ‘pearl,’ or even just ‘jewelry’.”

“I’ll have to do it in each file, but sure,” Detective Keymer said. He started to work his way down the list, clicking on files and then searching in them for the terms they were looking for. With each one, Maya felt the tension of a moment of expectation, followed by a brief flash of disappointment as he clicked onto the next file.

Then, finally, after what seemed like endless attempts, he didn’t.

“I’ve got a hit. Heather Sullivan, 25. She was killed maybe three months ago strangled at night in an alley and a moonstone was left on her body.”

“No one thought there was a connection?” Marco asked, sounding slightly incredulous that no one would have noticed it.

Detective Keymer shrugged, looking a little embarrassed. “It wasn’t the night of the full moon, so we never made the connection.”

And they’d already decided that it was the Moonlight Killer here in the police department.

The presence of the moonstone confirmed one thing though: there really was a serial killer here in Lagoon City, one with his own MO and motives, one who Maya needed to catch in the next two and a half days if she was going to stop another woman from dying at the Moonlight Killer’s hands.

CHAPTER ELEVEN

A part of Maya wanted to dive deep into the new case, exploring the death of Heather Sullivan in as much detail as possible. That would come in due course, but for now, she knew that they needed to keep going with the search through the records. If this truly was a serial killer, then there might potentially be far more than just two victims. She needed to know just how many of them there were.

"Check the rest of the files," Maya said to Detective Keymer. "We need to know exactly how many potential victims we're dealing with."

Marco nodded. "With a killer who's been operating for a year or more, there could be… that's potentially a lot of murders."

Maya swallowed at the thought of that. They didn't know how long this killer had been operating, or how frequently he killed. She suspected that one who had been operating for years and killing regularly would have been spotted by now even if the local PD didn't want to believe that there was any connection between the crimes, but it was still possible that there were many more victims out there that they hadn't spotted yet.

She could tell from the tension on Detective Keymer's face that he was thinking the same thing as he continued to work through the files, searching each one for any mention of pearls, moonstones, or jewelry. He scanned each carefully, and then moved on.

"Not this one," he said, pausing on a file. "This was just a robbery gone wrong, where a diamond necklace was taken." He kept looking through. "This one was an argument over an engagement ring that escalated into violence…"

That was the problem with the search: there were enough murders out there that were linked to robberies over jewelry such that they could potentially confuse things for them. The last thing Maya needed was to include anything that wasn't actually a part of the pattern, thus making the whole harder to decipher.

"I've got one more," Detective Keymer said, sounding anything but happy about it. "Dianne Smith, 24. She was killed just a couple of months ago."

"Are there any others?" Maya asked. Three was still plenty, confirming that they were dealing with a serial killer.

"No, that appears to be it."

Three murders in six months, all featuring young women in their twenties, all with moonstones left at the scene by the serial killer behind it. It was an obvious pattern, one that Maya was surprised the local police hadn't caught, but maybe they hadn't recognized that these were all moonstones, or that they had been left behind rather than being owned by the victims. Maya wanted to see what other connections there were.

"Can you send Marco and me the case files for all three victims?" she asked Detective Keymer.

He nodded. "Sending them across now."

"You're hoping that there will be a pattern that we can pick up on?" Marco asked.

"I am," Maya agreed. "There has to be a reason why he chose these women."

"He could just be copying the Moonlight Killer."

Maya shook her head. That didn't sound right, now that she had the details of more murders to work with. "Heather Sullivan wasn't killed on the full moon. Someone trying to copycat the Moonlight Killer would get that part right if nothing else. No, this is a separate killer, with his own motivations and methods. We need to work out what those are."

That meant looking at the three cases, the three women, and trying to establish what connections there were between them. Any connections they could find between the victims might point to a reason why the killer had targeted them and in turn help to lead back to him.

Maya set down her laptop on Detective Keymer's desk and started to look through the case files he sent over. Those files included crime scene reports, coroner's reports, and witness statements from the victims' families. Maya hoped that those would provide a good starting point, but whether they would be enough to go on was another question.

She had to bite back a wave of anger and horror at the sight of the crime scene photographs. The sight of the women lying there, abandoned as if they no longer mattered now that they were dead, was enough to disgust Maya and make her more determined that she was going to catch the man who had done this, whatever it took. She forced herself to pore over those photographs, taking in as many details as she could, trying to find whatever answers were there to find.

The more Maya looked, the more convinced she was that this was all the work of the same killer. The ligatures used for the strangulation were identical, while in the photographs, Maya could make out the faint gleam of moonstones left by the bodies. Now that Maya was looking for them, it was easy to see them for the calling cards they were, laying claim to the murders while speaking about some unknown agenda on the part of the killer.

Maya kept looking through the files while she called Samit. She would need tech support on this if she was going to establish a link between the victims. Their team's tech picked up quickly.

"Agent Gray, have you found anything?"

"Maybe," Maya said. She tried to work out how best to put it. "We've located a couple of other victims of this killer and now we need to know as much as possible about them. In particular we need to know if there are any connections between them."

"So you want me to look at call records and social media to see if there are any messages between any of them?" Samit guessed.

"Exactly." Maya was relieved that he'd gotten it so quickly. "I'd also like as much access as you can get me to the dead women's messages, so I can see if there was anyone making obvious threats towards any of them."

"Give me their names and I'll see what I can do," Samit said.

"Reba Andrews, Heather Sullivan, and Dianne Smith, all killed in the last six months. I'll send over their details."

"I'll get on it," Samit promised. "Agent Gray, I should say that Agent Harris has been here in the office again asking questions. He wants to know if we've gotten any closer to tracking down the kidnapper. When I told him that you were currently focusing on solving this case, he wasn't happy."

When was Harris ever happy with her work at the moment? He'd gone from thinking she was his star agent to wanting her taken off her own case. He thought that they should be more or less ignoring the cases the Moonlight Killer sent, going all out to track and capture him in his capacity as kidnapper. If Harris knew exactly who they were chasing, it would be even worse.

"I'll deal with Harris when I get back," Maya said. "For now, focus on getting me that information."

"On it," Samit said, hanging up.

That left Maya trying to think of other ways to find out more about the victims. She turned to Marco. "I'm going to try calling Heather Sullivan's family to find out if she knew any of the other victims. Can you do the same with Dianne Smith?"

She saw Marco nod. With almost anyone else, Maya would have felt the need to do this part of things herself, would have felt the need to control things, but Marco was good at this part of the job and Maya trusted him to ask the right questions. There was no one else she would rather have working with her right then.

She got the contact details for Heather Sullivan's next of kin, a sister, from the file. A part of Maya wondered if she should drive over to speak to her in person, but after the trip to Harrisburg, Maya was increasingly aware of how much of the day she and Marco had used up already chasing down the leads they had. If she could get the information she needed from a phone call, then that was the best way to go with all of this.

Punching in the number, Maya made the call and hoped that it would provide her with some answers.

"Hello?" a woman's voice asked on the other end of the line. "Who is this?"

"This is Agent Gray with the FBI," Maya said. "Am I speaking with Heather Sullivan's sister?"

There was a brief pause on the other end of the line, presumably as Heather's sister tried to decide if this was real or some kind of scam. Maybe a reporter trying to get information.

"I'm Geraldine Sullivan, yes," the woman said. "Does this mean… do you have any news about my sister? Have you caught the guy who did this to her?"

"Not yet," Maya said. "My partner and I work on cold cases. We've been assigned to this one." She didn't add that it had been by a psychopathic serial killer who was threatening the lives of innocent women if she didn't succeed. "It would be really helpful if you could tell me more about Heather."

"What do you want to know about her?" Geraldine asked.

Maya tried to get her questions into some kind of useful order. "For a start, did your sister own any pieces of moonstone jewelry?"

She had to eliminate the faint possibility that the moonstone was there coincidentally.

"No, I don't think so. Why?"

She sounded confused by the question.

"A piece was found at the scene, and I'm trying to establish if it was hers. Now, what was Heather like?"

"I'm sure everyone says this," Geraldine said, "but she was such a kind, nice person."

People often did switch to thinking better of the dead than they might have in life, but it wasn't universal.

"Can you think of anyone who might not have felt that way?" Maya asked. "Had she argued with anyone in the days before her death? Had anyone ever made threats towards her?"

"No, nothing like that," Geraldine replied, sounding shocked just by the prospect.

"Did your sister tell you about anything strange around her shortly before her death? Maybe she'd noticed someone paying her more attention than they should? Maybe she had a feeling that she was being watched?"

There was a brief pause on the other end of the line while Geraldine thought.

"No, I'm sorry. She didn't say anything like that. If she had, I would have told her to go to the police."

And the case file hadn't shown any sign of her reporting that kind of concern. Yet it seemed likely that the killer in this case would have stalked her before he made his kill. The fact that he'd known where to catch Reba Andrews alone suggested that he wasn't just picking a spot and waiting for someone to come by. So did the obvious similarities in age between the victims. He'd planned all of this.

"What did Heather do for a living?" Maya asked.

"She'd just gotten a new job," her sister replied. "She was going to start working as an overnight nurse."

Was it significant that her job would have kept her out at night, or did that just present a killer who liked to strike at night with the opportunity he needed?

"Did Heather ever mention knowing a woman named Reba Andrews?" Maya asked. "Or perhaps Dianne Smith?"

"I don't think I ever heard her use those names," Geraldine said. "Why? Are they involved in this?"

"I'm just exploring the possibility that your sister's death might be linked to another case," Maya said. "One last thing, can you think of anything now, any detail that you've thought of since the police interviewed you after your sister's death?"

"No, I'm really sorry. I wish I could tell you more." She sounded genuinely apologetic, like she'd been thinking about it for a while and feeling guilty.

"No, that's fine," Maya said. Even no information helped to confirm a few things at this stage. "Thank you for your time. If you do think of anything you can call me on this number at any time."

She hung up. Marco was waiting for her when she did so, obviously having finished his own call.

"Anything?" she asked him.

He shook his head. "Dianne Smith's family doesn't think she knew either of the others."

There was a message on her phone from Samit, too.

Nothing so far, will keep looking.

The combination was enough to suggest that the three women probably hadn't known one another in any meaningful way. That meant that whatever the connection between them that had made the killer target them rather than anyone else, it wasn't linked to their personal lives.

Could it just be down to them all fitting a victim type that the killer preferred? They were all women in their twenties, all in places at night that had allowed the killer to kill them without being seen. Maybe it was as simple as that, but Maya found herself hoping not.

If it was, then looking deeper into the lives of the victims wouldn't help Maya and Marco get any closer to the killer. That was frustrating enough to make Maya clench her fists, tight enough that her nails dug into her palms.

"We still have the moonstone angle," Marco said, obviously spotting that frustration.

That was true. If there was nothing to be found by looking at the victims, then the moonstones were their best chance, their *only* chance, as far as Maya could see.

They were going to have to talk to every jeweler and gem merchant they could find in the area. Someone, somewhere had sold those stones. If they could trace them, then they could find the killer.

CHAPTER TWELVE

There was something soothingly hypnotic about the rhythmical spinning of the rock tumbler. He watched it roll a piece of moonstone around and around, slowly polishing it, slowly starting to turn it into the representation of the moon that it was always meant to be.

The noise of the tumbling gemstone was constant and rhythmical, almost something to meditate upon, every fall around the tumbler's chamber accompanied by a rumbling clunk that seemed to produce a beat to match his heart.

It was almost exactly what he needed to relax; only one thing worked better, and it wasn't time for that yet. The moon wasn't up, wasn't at the perfect point in its endless cycle of creation and destruction, renewal and ending.

Was *he* a source of destruction? It was a question that bothered him sometimes in the build up to the moment when he killed those he had to kill. When he did what he had to do in order to bring about the change he required. Was he merely ending them, merely contributing to chaos and entropy with his actions? No, he didn't want to believe that. He was helping those who needed it to move on to another state of being, doing exactly what was required to release their energies beneath the endless cycle of the moon.

If he didn't, *that* would be chaos. The world, the whole universe, ran according to a natural order, one that neither he nor the women he killed could hope to upset.

Of course, they had tried to, first in trying to change their lives into something that the universe had not ordained for them, then at the moment of their release, by fighting against him. He tried to make it as painless as possible for them, not shedding their blood, taking only their breath from them with his garrote, but still, they seemed to want to fight him. They didn't see their place in the greater pattern of things.

He imagined that the next of them wouldn't see it either, wouldn't understand why what he was doing was necessary. He'd followed her off and on for days now, working out exactly where she would be under the moon's gaze, making sure that he would be able to do what was required in the perfect spot when the time came. Several times in the previous few days, he could have simply lunged forward and taken her, but that wasn't the point, that wasn't the way that this worked. He had to do this in the appointed place, at the appointed time.

It wasn't about the things he felt inside, urging him to kill them. It wasn't about the sense of peace he felt afterwards, or even the savage joy that was there in the last moments of their struggles. Those were distractions. If anything, they were signs that he hadn't gone far enough along his path yet.

He felt sure that the moon would free him from such needs if he went far enough, if he completed his work. If he did all that was required, if he freed enough from their earthly shells, then eventually he too would be free of it. He wasn't sure whether to delight in that possibility or fear it.

Would he be left with guilt at all he had done? He felt none now, but perhaps when all of this was done, he would feel its traces seeping into him. A part of him feared that, almost enough to put off what he had to do. He didn't want to feel the weight of guilt on his conscience, not when he was so blissfully free from it now. Guilt might drag him down, transform him, destroy him. It would tear him away from the path that he had so carefully embarked on. He was doing this to feel perfected, not imperfect.

Briefly, he left the rock tumbling machine to its work, heading up out of the basement that housed it, then out into the street. He drove to within a few hundred yards of the house that held his next victim, then got out so that he could approach closer on foot.

Was victim the right word? He was helping these women, not harming them. If they understood what he was trying to do, then he had no doubt that they would be grateful for it, only he didn't dare to stop and explain things to them once it was time to move them on from this existence. There was too much of a chance that they would fight back, that one of them would somehow stop him. That possibility was too terrible to contemplate.

Everything about this was pre-ordained: the person, the location, everything. There was nothing left to chance, because there *was* no chance, only the relentless pull of the universe, telling him what needed to be done.

He watched her for a while through her window. She was sitting at a piano, red-haired and lovely, young and full of potential. She was playing it, practicing, ahead of the gig he knew she had. The one that she thought was going to be her big break. The one that would place her at the perfect spot at the perfect time, the moon looking down on all of it.

He would be there then, exactly where he needed to be. He was always exact about where he needed to be because the placement mattered in this as much as the time. He would be waiting for her at the appointed hour, and she would come to him because fate would not allow anything else. She thought that she was changing her fate by going out on stage, but some things could not be changed.

At least, not without a special effort and the right rituals. Fate had force, had momentum. Overcoming it took more than just willing it. That was why he had to do this, exactly right. It was why the women he killed had to die.

Nothing would change otherwise.

CHAPTER THIRTEEN

"We need to find a jeweler," Maya said. "Quickly."

It was getting into evening as Maya and Marco hit the streets of the city, trying to talk to any jeweler they could. Detective Keymer had stayed behind at the police department, both to talk to the jeweler they'd left there and presumably to report everything to his bosses in the department.

That was fine by Maya; it meant that she and Marco could move quicker than they would have been able to with the detective slowing them down.

There was no fast way to do this, though, not that she could see. There was no overarching register of who had bought and sold what stones to whom, which meant that the two of them were going to have to talk to jewelers until they found one who had the information they needed.

They started with a jeweler's not far from the police precinct: a bright commercial place with rings and necklaces displayed prominently in the windows to catch the eye on black velvet backing. They sparkled there, obviously designed to draw the two of them in. Almost as soon as Maya and Marco stepped inside, a young woman working as a sales assistant stepped up to them, greeting them with a broad smile. She was maybe twenty, wearing a dark shirt and skirt, which served as the setting for a couple of tasteful pieces of jewelry of her own.

"Hi there," she said. "I'm Sidney. What are you looking for today? Perhaps a lovely necklace for the lady? A watch for the gentleman? Or…" her voice took on an almost conspiratorial note. "Have we reached the stage where we're shopping for rings?"

Maya looked over at Marco with a note of embarrassment made greater by the fact that they *were* in some kind of relationship. The two of them were *somewhere*, definitely something more than just partners by now, but they definitely weren't at that stage. Would they be, at some point? Could Maya imagine her and Marco settling down together somewhere?

It was surprisingly easy to do for a moment, but then Maya found herself thinking of Detective Keymer and his wife. They'd been partners and had settled down, then his wife had felt like she had to give up working in law enforcement. Maya wasn't sure if she could ever do something like that. She certainly didn't *want* that.

That was a thought for another time, though. For now, she had a job to do. Maya flashed her badge, making it clear that this was official.

"Agent Gray, FBI. I need to know if you've sold any moonstones to anyone in the last year."

"Moonstones?" the sales assistant said. "I don't think we get many of those through here. I'd have to check."

"Could you?" Marco said. "It's important that we know either way."

The sales assistant hurried off, leaving Maya and Marco with nothing better to do than stand there, staring at the stock on display. It ranged from very simple stud earrings all the way up to multi-piece chokers and even tiaras.

"This is… a lot," Maya said. Too much, certainly far more than she would ever wear.

"You're not a jewelry person?" Marco asked her.

Maya shrugged. "I don't really care one way or the other about it. When I was in the military, anything that shone or could catch on something was probably not a good idea. Now… well, it's pretty, I guess."

"You guess." Marco was smiling now, obviously making fun of her just a little.

"What? I'm just more of a… practical person."

"You're probably the most practical person I know," Marco agreed. "It's just one of your many good qualities."

Maya wasn't entirely certain whether he was making fun of her or not now. She *was* grateful when the store assistant came back, shaking her head.

"I'm sorry," the assistant said. "We don't really carry moonstones. They're kind of a specialist item. There might have been one in a bracelet, but that was close to two years ago."

Which was further back than Maya suspected the killer would have gone shopping for the stones he needed. It seemed likely that there would be some correlation between the acquisition of the stones and the start of the killing spree and two years was simply too long.

"Thank you anyway," Maya said. "Do you know of any jewelers who might stock moonstones?"

The store assistant shrugged. “Maybe Hansen’s, a couple of blocks over? It’s hard to say. Like I said, they’re kind of a specialist item. Moonstones are pretty rare.”

At least that gave them a clue about where to go next. They drove over to the jeweler’s and found it was a little smaller than the other store had been, with a sign saying that it had been in the same spot for at least the last fifty years.

When they went inside, there was an older man standing behind the store’s counter, looking as though he’d been there for most of the time that the store had been in business. He was white-haired with dark glasses, wearing a pinstripe suit with no tie.

Maya showed her badge almost as soon as she was in the store this time, not wanting to get stuck with this man thinking that she and Marco were shopping for engagement rings again.

“I’m Agent Gray, with the FBI,” she said, stepping up to the counter. “Are you the owner?”

“I’m Gregor Hansen, yes.”

“I’m looking for information on moonstones. Another jeweler said that it was possible you might sell them.”

Mr. Hansen nodded. “We have a couple of pieces containing them, certainly. Antique pieces, with authentic clear blues from Myanmar.”

“Have you sold many pieces like that in the past couple of years?” Marco asked.

“What’s this about?” Mr. Hansen asked. “All my gemstones are sourced legally. I have the paperwork to prove it.”

Maya realized that he thought they were there for him, to interfere with his business. She hurried to correct him. “We’re here because several moonstones have been left at the scenes of crimes my partner and I are investigating as a kind of calling card.”

That seemed to catch Mr. Hansen’s interest. “Just the stones? Not with a piece of jewelry?”

Maya nodded. “That’s right. Single stones. Round, like pearls.”

“Then I’m not sure if I can help you. I don’t sell individual stones.”

“Is it possible that someone could have removed moonstones from pieces of jewelry?” Marco asked. “Just pried them out in order to use it?”

Mr. Hansen looked disturbed by the possibility. “I suppose someone *could*. Although the pieces I sell typically have only one stone. You implied that there were multiple such stones found.”

That was true. Someone would need to buy a lot of moonstone pieces to have the kind of supply the killer would want for his murders. Was that a practical way for the killer to go about it?

"Have you sold multiple moonstone pieces to the same person?" Maya asked him.

Mr. Hansen shook his head. "I get relatively small numbers of pieces in. I would remember if one person had bought several. I'm sorry."

Which meant that they were in the wrong place. Again. Maya made to leave.

"One thing," Mr. Hansen said. "If you're looking for stones that haven't been set, it may not be a jeweler you need. For that, I would go to a gemstone dealer who trades in such things."

That caught Maya's attention. It potentially pointed them in the right direction, potentially saved them a lot of time that they would otherwise spend going from jeweler to jeweler, trying to find an answer.

"Do you know of any gem dealers who deal in moonstones?" Maya asked.

She saw Mr. Hansen nod. "I believe I can point you in the right direction. Although whether you'll be able to get him to talk to you about his pieces is another matter. He values his privacy."

He wrote down details on a scrap of paper, passing it over to Maya. It held an address and a name: Nils Schafer.

Maya and Marco headed outside. It was starting to get darker now and Maya was grateful that the jeweler had given them a direction to go in while they still had some time left in the day. Even so, they were going to have to hurry, because Maya imagined that a gem dealer wouldn't stay open all night.

She and Marco drove over. It wasn't far, but even so, Maya found herself hoping that they would be in time. She didn't want to start over with this in the morning when there was still a chance of making progress tonight.

It turned out that she needn't have worried about it. The address Mr. Hansen had provided turned out to be a private house, a large townhouse with a view out over one of the many lakes around the city and with a large BMW parked outside. Everything about the place screamed wealth.

As Maya approached the door, though, she saw that it was a lot more than just a normal house. There were security cameras looking down at her and the door looked as though it could have withstood a battering ram. There was an intercom there and Maya pressed the buzzer.

"Hello?" a man's voice said, after a moment or two of them waiting. "Do you have an appointment?"

Maya held up her badge for one of the cameras to see. "I'm Agent Gray, with the FBI, this is my partner, Detective Spinelli. Can we talk to you about moonstones?"

"If you want to talk to me about something connected with my business, you'll have to make contact through my attorney."

It was a kind of professional defensiveness that seemed anything but personal. Maya couldn't work out if it was just a reflex, or if he was actually trying to hide something.

She guessed that there might be an element of the latter, so that the only way to get in to talk to the gem dealer would be if he was sure that they weren't going to look too closely at his business dealings.

"We're here about a murder, Mr. Schafer, not about your business," Maya said. "We only want to talk."

"I'm not involved in any murder, and I don't want to be."

"We don't think you're involved in the murder, Mr. Schafer. We just need your professional expertise." The more Maya could make this sound like they needed him as an expert witness, the better.

There was a pause on the other end of the intercom, one that stretched out over several seconds and left Maya wondering if she and Marco were just going to be left out there. Instead though, the door opened slowly, letting them into a hallway with a red and white chequerboard floor, a golden chandelier hanging overhead. There were artworks on the wall that Maya didn't recognize, but which looked expensive, nevertheless.

A broad shouldered man in his fifties was waiting for them as they entered the house. He was wearing a dark suit with a diamond tie pin. Another, larger man stood behind him, and Maya could make out the bulge of the gun beneath his jacket. Maya guessed that he was a bodyguard.

"I'm Nils Schafer. You'd better come through to my office." He gestured for the two of them to follow him, turning sharply on his heel. He led the way to a second steel security door, which he opened with a key, revealing a wood paneled office space within. There was a broad mahogany desk there dominating one side of it, with expensively engineered seats on either side of it and a sleek laptop in the middle. A third security door sat at the back of the office, presumably leading to some kind of vault.

The gem dealer took a seat on the far side of the table, while his security guard took up a station near the door, just on the edge of Maya's vision. Maya kept half an eye on him automatically, but most of her attention was on Nils Schafer.

"Mr. Schafer," Maya said. "Do the gemstones you sell include moonstones?"

"Sometimes," Schafer said, spreading his hands. "Why?"

Maya considered how much to tell him. There was no point in holding anything back now, though, not when she'd already told him that this was in connection with a murder.

"Several women have been killed," Maya said. "A moonstone was left at each scene. We're hoping that we might be able to trace those moonstones."

"My clients value my discretion," Schafer said, with a perfect poker face that promised no way in.

"Even when one of those clients might be murderer?" Marco asked.

Schafer hesitated for another moment or two. Now, the faintest of cracks showed in his expression.

"We only want to know if someone has bought a batch of moonstones from you in the last year," Maya said. "We're not looking for your commercial details, or for details of their private lives. Just a name that might help to lead us to a killer."

"My business is built on my reputation," Schafer said. "That is valuable to me."

Marco stepped in then, without any give in his tone. "And how will that reputation stand up once we start to go through your business affairs? Will people want to be associated with a business under investigation by the FBI?"

Maya didn't like that they had to resort to threats, but right then, it seemed like the only way they were going to get any answers. Given how little time they had, she would do anything she needed to do. Besides, she could see just how uncomfortable it made the gem dealer.

"All right, all right," he said. "I'll check. But you didn't get any of this from me, understood?"

Maya nodded. Schafer opened up his computer, typing something in while being careful not to let them see the screen. He was being very careful about protecting his clients' information.

"Moonstones… yes. I thought there were. I sold a batch of moonstones to a client named Aldo Weber about eight months back. Half a dozen stones, all high quality. There, is that what you want to know?"

“Thank you,” Maya said.
“Then get out of my house.”

CHAPTER FOURTEEN

It took another hour for Maya and Marco to get a warrant from a friendly judge to search Aldo Weber's home for the moonstones. Actually, it was mostly Marco who did the work of getting the warrant, rushing off to convince the judge that the link to the moonstones was enough for them to consider Weber a serious suspect.

Maya took the time to research him while Marco went to get the warrant, and was surprised to find that he had a record of violence, along with a couple of arrests. One had been for a fight with a former employee, another for an attack on a then girlfriend that had included putting his hand around her throat. That was a detail that made Maya instantly more suspicious.

In both cases, though, the victims declined to press charges in spite of what appeared to be clear evidence against him. Maya suspected that some kind of payoff or threat might have been involved. It only made Maya feel it was more likely that this was the killer. A man with a history of violence, used to getting away with it, who had bought a batch of moonstones just a couple of months before seemed like a very good fit indeed.

They drove over to his house: a large two-story place in the middle of broad, nicely landscaped gardens. There was a large SUV outside, along with a sports car. Marco pulled up behind them, obviously trying to slow Weber down a little if he tried to escape. Maya was glad that she had someone with her who was tactically aware, who she could trust to watch her back without worrying that he was going to put her or himself in danger.

They got out, approaching the door. Maya made sure that her gun was ready to draw. She'd had people attack her before as she approached their homes and the killers she'd taken down had all fought hard to keep from being arrested.

She approached the door while Marco stood slightly off to one side, ready to back her up if anything happened. Maya rang the bell, waiting for an answer from within. Maya fully expected one. There were lights on in the house and the cars were there in the driveway, so she guessed that someone was home.

There was no answer from inside though, so Maya switched to hammering on the door. "Aldo Weber! This is the FBI! Open up!"

It was important to identify herself. Either to get Weber to comply or just to get a reaction from him. If he tried to run, even that would be something.

There still wasn't an answer, though. Maya looked over to Marco. "Break it down."

"You're sure?" Marco asked, sounding a little worried about the prospect.

Maya nodded. "We have a warrant and he's refusing to answer. So we break it down and *make* him answer."

She saw Marco take a step back and then he kicked out, the crunch of his booted foot against the door loud against the night. He kicked again and now the lock broke, the door swinging open to let them inside. The interior of the house was clean and elegant, with hardwood floors and gray painted walls. Statues sat here and there, each individually lit.

Maya had her gun out now, because if Weber hadn't answered, there was a chance that he was lying in wait for them, ready to ambush them. She moved through the house, checking for danger as she went, with Marco moving alongside her.

They went through into a broad lounge with French windows looking out onto the gardens. Maya realized with a start that the lake where Reba had been found was just visible in the distance. She had to snap her attention back to the room, though. It was cluttered with furniture, a couple of tables taking up space, a desk in the corner set up as a workstation. There was a broad white couch along one wall, along with an armchair set in front of a huge TV, which was currently blaring out with an action movie.

Aldo Weber was there, watching the movie. He was a tall, slender man, casually dressed in jeans and a dark shirt. He spotted them as they came into the room and Maya saw his eyes widen. She knew a second before he did it that he was going to dive for cover, but by then it was too late to stop him from doing it.

Weber flung himself out of his chair, diving down behind one of the tables there. He came up, a gun in his hands, firing blindly.

Now it was Maya's turn to dive for cover, throwing herself over the top of the couch to land behind it. Marco appeared next to her a moment later, firing back over the top of the sofa.

Weber was running now. Maya popped up, ready to take the shot if he turned to fire, but instead, he seemed to have dropped his gun, so that it skidded across the hardwood floor. Maya got the impression that he didn't know what he was doing with it, because who would just abandon their weapon in the middle of a firefight.

Maya had no time to get an answer to that question, though, because she was busy trying to catch up. He was running through the house now, making his way out into the hall. Maya thought that maybe he was trying to get outside, but no, he seemed to be heading upstairs instead.

"FBI, freeze!" Maya called out, but Weber gave no sign of stopping.

Instead, he ran upstairs with surprising speed, outpacing Maya's efforts to follow him as he headed for one of the bedrooms there at the top of the stairs. Was he trying to get to another weapon? Did he have an escape route that way? Maya didn't know, but she *did* know that she couldn't afford to let him get any further ahead of her. She sprinted after him, trying to catch up before he got to wherever he was going.

Maya burst into a bedroom, just in time for Weber to knock over a clothes rail, sending it tumbling right into Maya's path. Maya vaulted it, but her foot snagged for a moment on one of the shirts there so that she could only stand and try to disentangle it as Weber headed for a patch of wall…

It swung open at his touch, a thick steel door swinging open to reveal a room within. Weber dove inside and Maya realized that it wasn't an escape route he was trying to get to but a panic room.

Finally disentangling her foot from the shirt, Maya lunged at him, but the door was already swinging closed. Maya tried to get her fingers inside the door to pull it open, but the hydraulics closing it were far too strong to fight against. Maya barely jerked her fingers back in time to avoid losing them as it swung shut with an audible click, leaving her staring at a blank patch of wall again.

"Damn it!" Maya snapped, trying to see a way in. There wasn't one. Of course there wasn't because that was the *point* of a panic room. If it were easy to get into, then it wouldn't be doing its job.

Marco was there then, just a couple of paces behind her. Maya had been so focused on Weber during the chase that she hadn't been able to keep track of him.

"What happened?" Marco asked. "Where did he go?"

"He's in a panic room just here," Maya said, touching the wall where the door sat, trying to find the edges of it. There would be a way in, but Maya wasn't sure what that would be yet.

"A panic room?" Marco said. "So where does that leave us? Do we just wait him out?"

"For now," Maya replied. "We also need to find a way of contacting him to try to talk him out of there and maybe get onto the company that installed this to see if there's a way in there that might let us get to him."

"If it's well built, then short of tearing the whole house apart it's unlikely to work," Marco pointed out.

"If that's what's needed," Maya shot back. She wasn't going to let Weber just sit in there to evade justice.

The worst case scenario was one she didn't want to contemplate, in which he just sat inside that room for the next few days. They might eventually starve him out, but the deadline would be long past by then.

"I'll call Keymer," Maya said. "See if we can get some additional cops here to cover the exits. After that, we'll start working out how to get him out of there. I'll also search the house to see if there's any sign of the moonstones. Keep an eye on this door in the meantime so that he has no chance to escape."

"Will do," Marco promised.

Maya headed out of the bedroom, moving downstairs. She got out her phone to call Keymer.

"Keymer, it's Agent Gray," she said as he picked up. "I need you to send some uniforms over to my location, to assist in securing it. Our suspect is here, but he's holed up and it doesn't look like…"

Maya trailed off as she saw movement outside. Her heart went into overdrive as she saw three men approaching, rifles in their hands.

"Marco, stay up there and call for help. We've got company."

She had an instant to draw her gun and move into cover behind a corner, before a trio of heavily armed men burst in, wearing full tactical gear. Their weapons were trained on the spot where she was hiding in an instant.

"Drop your weapon!" one bellowed at her.

"I'm FBI!" she shouted back at him.

"That's not what our client says. He says this is a home invasion. Now throw out your weapon. I won't ask again."

Maya didn't throw out her gun. She wasn't going to give it up that easily, but she *did* send her badge spinning across the floor towards the feet of the man who'd spoken. She followed it up a moment later with her warrant.

"I'm FBI," Maya repeated, "and I have a warrant to search this place. When your client refused to answer the door, we forced entry and he started shooting at us. What are you, private security?"

"We protect our clients from threats," the one who was doing the talking said.

"Well, what about the legal threat that comes from all of you pointing weapons at an FBI agent?" Maya demanded. From her hiding place, she watched the leader look at the badge and read the warrant over. She also found herself praying that Marco wouldn't come bursting in to try to save her. At this point, it would be like throwing a match into the middle of a dry forest.

"Stand down," the leader said after what seemed like forever. "She's legit."

The three lowered their weapons. Maya moved out of her cover slowly, ready to dive back if there was any sign of the weapons coming back up.

"Sorry to inconvenience you, Agent," the leader said. "We had to react to the threat. I'm sure you understand."

Maya understood that these men were just doing their job, but her heart was still pounding with what had just almost happened. Even so, her mind was still able to focus enough to pick up on one detail of the brief conversation she'd just had with them.

"You said that he told you this was a home invasion?"

"That's right, ma'am."

"Meaning that you have a means of communicating with him?" Maya said.

"Yes ma'am."

"Then for his sake, tell him that we *are* the FBI, that this isn't a home invasion, and that he needs to come out."

The security specialist hesitated, then passed her badge and warrant back to her. "I'll see what I can do."

Maya headed back upstairs. One of the security guys went with her, which meant that Maya spent the whole time watching for any sudden movements. She needn't have worried. By the time they reached the bedroom, Aldo Weber was already coming out of his hiding place, looking slightly terrified by the whole thing.

Right then, Maya didn't have a lot of sympathy for him.

"Aldo Weber? You're under arrest."

CHAPTER FIFTEEN

Maya watched Aldo Weber with his lawyer discussing his situation in the interrogation room side by side at a desk there, staring at them through the one way glass. The lawyer looked expensive, middle-aged, sharp-suited, and not at all happy to be in a police precinct at this hour of the night. Maya was impatient to get in there, but of course, Weber had lawyered up the moment they'd gotten back to the precinct.

"It's all right," Marco said. "He's not going anywhere."

Trust Marco to pick up on the tension she felt at not being able to get in there. He knew her probably as well as anyone did now. He knew things about her that no one else did.

"It's just like I can feel the seconds ticking away," Maya said. "We've used up almost all of our first day."

"And we have a solid suspect in there to interrogate," Marco said, "while a CSI team is down at Weber's house, searching it for the moonstones. We've done a lot in one day, Maya."

Maya just hoped that it was going to be enough. If this was the killer, and if they could prove that, then they were well ahead of schedule, yet every delay still made her feel as though they were inching closer to a woman's death at the hands of the Moonlight Killer.

Finally, the lawyer indicated that he and his client were ready, waving them in with the confidence of someone who knew that they would be watching from the other side of the one-way glass.

Maya went in there with Marco at her side. The lawyer gestured to the desk he and Weber were sitting at, as if inviting Maya and Marco to sit down. He was obviously used to getting his way in situations involving the authorities.

"My client wishes to make it clear," the lawyer said. "That what happened tonight was all a big misunderstanding."

"One in which he shot at members of the FBI," Maya pointed out. "We were there to execute a search warrant and he fired at us."

"He believed that he was in the middle of a home invasion," the lawyer said. "He reacted as any reasonable person might have in that situation."

"We identified ourselves as FBI," Maya said.

"My client didn't hear you, and even if he had, he would have had every reason to believe that it was some trick to get him to hold still long enough for you to kill or abduct him."

The lawyer said it in flat tones that allowed for no dispute.

Maya was willing to give in on all the points the lawyer had made in principle, but for now, she didn't want to concede them, simply because she wanted to have as many reasons to hang on to Weber as possible until they got to the truth.

"I'm more interested in the possibility that your client has murdered at least three women," Maya said. She watched Weber's expression as she said it, taking in the sudden horror that crossed his features. Was that horror at being caught, or just at the thought of someone accusing him like that?

"Killed someone?" Weber said. "You think I *killed* someone?"

Maya nodded. "Three people. Three women. Do the names Reba Andrews, Heather Sullivan, and Dianne Smith mean anything to you?"

Weber shook his head immediately. "Of course not."

The lawyer stepped in. "Is there any reason why you're harassing my client like this? Do you have any *evidence* linking him to these crimes?"

Marco asked the next question. "Is it true that you bought a batch of moonstones eight months ago?"

"We're jumping from accusations of murder to my client's shopping habits?" the lawyer demanded, leaning forward in his seat.

Maya knew that he was trying to make everything that she and Marco had come up with sound like it was nothing. She wasn't going to allow him to deflect attention that easily.

"Moonstones were found at the sites of the murders," Maya said. "From what we've learned, those aren't very common. Only a few jewelers in town have any pieces at all, while *you,* Aldo, bought a whole batch of them, right before the first murder took place."

"I bought those for a client!" Weber protested. "That's what I do. I locate unique things for wealthy people. That sports car on my driveway, it's a one off that's going to an NBA star in two days. A client wanted some moonstones, so I *found* him some moonstones."

Was he telling the truth? Everything about his demeanor suggested that he was, while the nature of his business wouldn't be hard to check. Maya looked over to Marco and gestured to the door.

The two of them headed out of the interrogation room, only to find Detective Keymer waiting there for them. Marco started to look up

Weber's business on his phone while Maya gave the detective her attention.

"I've just had a call from the CSI team," Keymer said. "There's no sign of any moonstones on the property."

That was worrying news. Assuming that the killer wasn't done, and a serial killer like the one they were dealing with here wouldn't stop so easily, then he would need to have a supply of moonstones close at hand. Maya and Marco had found out firsthand just how difficult they were to obtain in Lagoon City, so it wasn't as if the killer could just go out and buy one whenever he needed it.

It was still possible, though, that Weber was lying. He might have the moonstones stashed somewhere else, ready to pick them up to use in the murders.

It seemed that Marco was getting somewhere with his research, though.

"Weber's business is what he describes," Marco said. "He's basically a fixer, finding things for rich people and taking a cut. His story about moving the moonstones on to someone else makes sense."

That was frustrating, because it increased the likelihood that they were going in the wrong direction with all of this. Still, Maya wasn't about to let it go that easily. There were other things she needed to check. She headed back into the interrogation room.

Weber and his lawyer were waiting there, each of them looking slightly smug in his own way, as if they were both certain that the whole situation was going to resolve to their satisfaction.

Maya wrote down the dates of the three murders, pushing the paper across the table towards Weber.

"What's this?" his lawyer demanded.

"Where was your client on these three evenings?" Maya demanded.

"You really expect him to remember where he was on evenings months in the past?" the lawyer shot back.

Maya shrugged. "If he wants to get this cleared up, then he'll check."

To Maya's surprise, Weber didn't look bothered as he stared at the dates. Instead, he looked more than a little relieved.

"I don't know about the other two, but for this middle one I was in France, brokering a deal with a fashion house for a couple of their earliest pieces. I kept the travel tickets for my expenses, and there are pictures of me there."

In just a few words, any hope that they'd caught the killer faded away. If he had an alibi for even one of the murders, then it wasn't him.

This was a serial killer, so anyone they caught had to have been able to commit all three murders. The idea that there was more than one killer leaving moonstones behind simply asked too much of coincidence.

Weber's lawyer stood. "Now that we've resolved that, my client and I will be leaving."

Maya was almost tempted to just let them go, writing the whole thing off as a giant mistake, but there were still things she needed to know.

"Not yet."

"Agent Gray," the lawyer said. "We have just established that my client cannot be the killer you're looking for. Continuing to hold him after that amounts to harassment and wrongful arrest."

That was probably a bluff, but Maya imagined that it was one that would work with a lot of people. Not her, though. Not when her sister's life hung in the balance, resting on whether she found the killer in this case in time.

"Sit down, Weber," Maya said. "You said that you bought the moonstones for a client. Who was that?"

She saw Weber shake his head. "I can't tell you that." He seemed almost as horrified at that prospect as he had been to be accused of murder. "My clients expect confidentiality."

"Well, maybe you'd like to sit here and think about that for a while," Maya said.

The lawyer didn't look happy about that. "You cannot do this, Agent Gray. We have established that my client is innocent, so you have no business continuing to hold him."

The frustrations of the day had been piling up inside Maya. The fact that Weber and his lawyer were trying to hold her back now was the last straw.

"Your client shot at a federal agent," Maya said. "We had a search warrant, and we identified ourselves. I don't care about his excuses; he did that. Now, unless he wants to face the full consequences of it, then he needs to start talking about who he sold the moonstones to. That client could be our killer."

Even now, Maya could see Weber hesitating. He had an urgent, whispered conversation with his lawyer. It was the lawyer who finally spoke.

"My client is prepared to be open with you about *his* client, if you are prepared to let the little… misunderstanding at his house drop."

It was the quickest way for Maya to get the answers she wanted, so she was prepared to go along with it.

"Ok," she said. "What's the name, Aldo?"

Weber looked over at her with obvious dislike. "I sold the moonstones to a man named Henrique Garner, but if you think he had anything to do with this, you're crazy."

"That's something we'll have to determine," Maya said.

"No, I'm telling you," Weber insisted. "Garner lives in Hawaii. Doesn't travel out of state. That's part of why he hires me to find things for him. He flatly refuses to leave. He's never even *been* to Lagoon City."

Just like that, Maya felt as though the bottom had dropped out of all her hopes. She'd thought that following the moonstones would lead her back to the killer, but now it seemed that they led to a man who had no chance of being the one they were looking for. She and Marco would check Garner to make sure that Weber was telling the truth, but if he was, then they'd just hit a dead end, one that had cost them an entire day of the three that they had to find the killer.

They had to find another lead now, and they only had two days left before the Moonlight Killer made good on his threat to kill one of his hostages. Perhaps it would even be Megan.

Maya walked out of the interrogation room, determined to find out what that lead would be. Marco was waiting for her.

"It looks like we're done here," Marco said. "A quick search says that Garner is famously a recluse. It's not him."

"We still need to check flight records, and-"

Marco caught her arms. "It's not him, Maya. I know you're pushing hard for this, but we don't have any more time today."

Maya shook her head. She didn't want to admit that, didn't want to give in. "We only have three days, Marco. Two now."

"And you won't be able to make the most of those remaining days if you exhaust yourself today chasing after something that isn't there," Marco pointed out.

Maya knew that was true, but even so, she hated it.

"We need to call it a day," Marco said. "We need to find somewhere to stay, then start fresh in the morning."

Maya nodded. She hated having to give in on this, but she knew that Marco was right. One thing was certain, though, first thing tomorrow, they were going to start fresh and try to find answers.

Maya just hoped that there were some answers out there for them to find.

CHAPTER SIXTEEN

Laney sat at the piano in front of the audience at the club, letting the notes spill out of her. The shine of the house lights reflected from the piano's patina, making it seem as if she were playing in the midst of a wash of light. The waxing moon spilled off the lake outside, so that it was hard to tell where the water finished and the interior of the club began.

When she looked up, she could see the audience there at their tables, enjoying their night out. Not huge numbers, because this was a first gig, but still plenty of them. More than that, they seemed to be enjoying themselves; that was the main thing.

Around Laney, the club's band played, the drummer and the double bass player forming a groove so solid that it gave her the freedom to drift and improvise, her fingers seeming to fly in response to the harmony. Laney kept playing, letting the music rise and fall, playing with the dynamics and the tone.

A year ago, she wouldn't have dared to do this. She'd been stuck in her job as a librarian, existing but not really living, only playing her piano in the privacy of her own home. Then a boyfriend had told her that she was hiding from her life, not doing what she really wanted to do. The advice had stuck; the boyfriend hadn't.

Laney had thrown herself into practice, all in preparation for tonight. Tonight was her debut, her big chance to make an impression in the local music scene. She'd been so nervous going into tonight, the stage fright almost threatening to overwhelm her. That fear had still been there right up until the moment when she'd played the first few notes.

After that, the music had taken over, until now it was the only thing. Laney could feel the ebb and flow of it, building to the perfect climax…

She hit the last chord, let it linger, and then stood while applause washed over her. In that moment, it didn't matter that she was in a club in Lagoon City rather than in front of a thousand people in a big hall somewhere. What mattered was that she felt more alive than she had in forever.

Laney went up to hug the two members of the house band.

“You did great,” the drummer said. “I loved the polyrhythms you played with in the last chorus.”

“You’re good,” the bassist said. “We’d better see you again here.”

“You will,” Laney promised them, as she rushed offstage and the next person who wanted to sit in with the house band came up. Laney felt as though she was walking on clouds, as though everything was perfect in that moment.

A couple more people stopped to congratulate her, but Laney barely took it all in. She was still high on the applause and the feeling of the music. That feeling carried her all the way to the stage door and the night air beyond.

Laney breathed it in, staring up at the stars. It felt as if she could reach out and touch them right then. They were reflected in the lake that sat beyond the club, so that Laney found herself counting those too. It felt as if she didn’t want this night to end. Laney started to make her way along the lakeshore, back to her waiting car.

She was halfway along it when she spotted something small and shining there in a corner, behind a couple of rocks, glimmering in the moonlight. Laney bent down to see what it was and saw some kind of highly polished gemstone that someone had just abandoned there. Not knowing what to make of it, Laney picked it up, examining it in the light.

Laney was still doing that when she heard the sound of footsteps approaching along the shoreline. She turned towards them. Maybe it was whoever had dropped the stone, coming to look for it. Maybe it was someone from the club who had come to tell her that they’d enjoyed her performance. Her imagination was filled then with thoughts of R&D people who just happened to be in the right place at the right time to spot her.

“Is there anybody there?” Laney asked. She thought she saw a flash of movement, there in the dark.

Now more worrying possibilities came to her and Laney felt a thrill of fear. It was enough to make her hurry towards her car. She risked a glance back along the shore and saw a figure there, moving forward quickly. In the dark, it was impossible to make out more than that.

Laney turned to run, determined to get to her car and safety. She sprinted towards it, trying to get there. It was just ahead. Laney started to fish for her keys in her purse, trying to open the door.

She was still fumbling for them when the rope dropped around her throat, and she was torn from her feet…

CHAPTER SEVENTEEN

Maya had done it. She'd worked out the clues in the postcards. She'd unraveled all the secrets holding her back. She knew where the Moonlight Killer was.

A cabin stood ahead, across a field of gamboling bunny rabbits. Maya crossed it carefully, keeping her gun out, knowing that danger might be coming for her at any moment. She took out the last postcard, checking the picture of the cabin on it; it was the same. She kept moving across the field.

She froze, her heart pounding, as her foot brushed up against a tripwire. She stepped over it, tiptoeing across the field now because it seemed like the only way to avoid traps.

The bunnies scattered as Maya approached the cabin, leaving her alone there on the doorstep. She took a breath, tried the door, and slipped inside. She cleared the room expertly, the cozy surroundings of the cabin far too homespun considering the killer they hid.

When Maya spotted the trapdoor, she understood. She threw it open and climbed down into a tunnel lit by a series of flickering strip lights. Those lights seemed to flicker in sequence away from Maya, drawing her on, deeper into the place.

Finally, she came out into a large circular chamber, where women were being held in cages, locks stopping them from getting out. Maya shot those locks one by one, not caring now if someone heard. Maya *wanted* the Moonlight Killer to come to her.

He did. He appeared on the other side of the room from a doorway Maya hadn't seen before, wearing all black, a mask covering his face. Even through it, Maya could sense the hatred there.

He charged and Maya fired on instinct, pulling the trigger again and again, not stopping until the clip of her gun was empty. The Moonlight Killer went down, sprawled in a pool of blood, looking far less intimidating now that Maya had stopped him.

She rushed forward, grabbing for his mask, tearing it from his face…

Her sister's features stared back at her, her eyes staring and accusing.

"Maya…"

"Maya! Wake up!"

Maya woke up in a cold sweat, the light of the waxing moon streaming in through her hotel window. It was still the middle of the night.

"Maya, are you there?" She heard Marco's voice coming from the other side of the door. They'd settled on two rooms for tonight, although it would have been easy not to.

Maya got up in her pajamas and hurried to the door. Marco was there waiting for her. There were plenty of circumstances in which she would have loved to find Marco waiting at her bedroom door. From the look on his face, though, this wasn't like that. There was no look of barely repressed passion, only an expression of worry.

"Are you ok?" Marco asked her as she opened the door. "You were crying out in your sleep."

Maya waved that away. "Bad dream, that's all."

She didn't want to go into the details of that bad dream, or what it said about her deepest fears. Maya already knew what the dream meant: she was terrified that, at the end of all of this, all that might be waiting was her sister's death.

"Did you wake me up just because I was having a nightmare?" Maya asked. Had she really been loud enough to wake Marco up like that?

"I wish it were just that," Marco said. Maya realized then that he was fully dressed, ready to go like it was already the next morning.

"What is it?" Maya asked.

"I just had a call from Detective Keymer," Marco said. "Another body has just been found with a moonstone on top of it."

*

The first thing that Maya noticed as they pulled up around the back of one of Lagoon City's clubs was that it was on a lake. Was that a connection in the cases, or was it simply that everything here was close to a lake? Maya didn't know.

The second thing she saw was the local police department containing the crime scene, pushing back a small crowd of onlookers along with a few local press. Maya approached quickly, stepping right past the police tape there with her badge already out for the uniformed officer on crowd control to see.

Keymer was there, standing close to the edge of the water and there, at his feet was the body of a young woman.

Maya couldn't help a moment of simply staring. It didn't matter that she was a seasoned FBI agent who had worked on many murder investigations. It didn't matter that she was ex-military intelligence and had seen her share of bodies back in conflict zones, that first moment of seeing the dead always hit her hard.

In this case, the deceased was a red-haired young woman, obviously in her early twenties, with skin that looked particularly pale in the moonlight. She was wearing a black cocktail dress and a short jacket. She lay sprawled out, as if she'd been abandoned where she fell, while her hands were curled up claw-like, as if she'd tried to scratch her way free of the assault that had killed her. A ligature was still wrapped around her neck, abandoned there by the killer.

A single moonstone shone just out of the dead woman's reach, sitting there in front of her as if to draw her towards it. It shone in a mixture of silver and blue under the moonlight. Its presence confirmed the connection to this case, but also showed again the difference between this killer's work and that of the Moonlight Killer.

Detective Keymer looked troubled by it all. He probably wasn't used to dealing with the work of a serial killer.

"What do we have, Keymer?" Maya asked him.

The detective gestured to the body, which the coroner's people were just getting ready to move.

"This is Laney Jackson, twenty-four years old. She lives across town."

"So what is she doing here?" Maya asked. "Did she just come to the club? Is it a place she comes regularly?"

If it wasn't, then they would have to change the way they were thinking about the killer. Currently, Maya was working off the assumption that the killer picked out specific targets and then worked out how best to ambush them, but if this wasn't a place he could have known Laney would come, then that swung things back in the direction of him being a more opportunistic killer. Maya wasn't sure which was more worrying. At least a killer who stalked his victims beforehand had a pattern that they might be able to trace back to him.

"We're still questioning people in and around the bar," Keymer said. "But it looks as though Laney came here to take part in some kind of gig. Jazz." He added that as if it made a difference to the way things had happened here.

"So she was a musician?" Maya said.

There was a time when she'd assumed that the kidnapper who'd taken her sister, the Moonlight Killer, liked to target creative types.

Now she knew different, but did this killer? Maybe he was still trying to copycat the Moonlight Killer as much as possible.

"She played piano," Keymer said. "Tonight was her debut."

Her debut? Maya turned to Marco, standing just behind her, taking in the crime scene. She was sure that the significance of that wouldn't be lost on him. They'd established several times now that the Moonlight Killer liked to kill people on the brink of a change in their lives, but Maya couldn't say that aloud now, not without a discussion of how exactly she'd worked it out.

"What do you see?" Maya asked Marco instead. He had more experience working live cases than Maya did, given that her background was in cold cases. Although she was starting to get her share of experience now.

"There's not much cover this way," Marco said. "So the killer would have approached from the direction of the bar and followed her in this direction. But if this is a pre-planned spot, then he must have known that Laney would come this way. There's something else, too. Why this particular spot? He could have killed her a lot closer to the bar without being seen, and that would have made it easier to get into position, hiding in the crowds. Here, he had to wait alone and risk discovery."

Meaning that this location was important to him somehow. It also meant something else.

"You're right," Maya said. "He had to know which way Laney would come."

"A car registered to her is in that direction," Detective Keymer said, gesturing.

Maya nodded. "Marco, check back towards the club, see if there's anything that might point us in the right direction. I'll go along towards the car and do the same."

"Got it," Marco said and set off.

Maya did the same, heading up the shoreline, keeping her eyes peeled for anything that might help them to find the killer. Maya wasn't sure if there would be anything since she suspected that the local CSI units would have already checked, but she couldn't leave it to chance.

Maya headed out quickly, trying not to draw attention to herself as she worked. The last thing she needed right then was a crowd of reporters watching her every move. With cold cases, it usually wasn't such a problem, but with a fresh kill there was definitely the potential for a media storm.

As she walked, she found herself wondering about the fact that there had been another murder. Why? Specifically, why *now*? That question bugged Maya as she walked. Was it just a coincidence that another murder had happened as she and Marco had come into town, or was the killer reacting to their presence? Had he seen somewhere on the news that the FBI had come into town and reacted to it? Was this his way of boasting to them that no one was able to stop him?

If so, was the fact that a woman was dead at least partly due to Maya? That was a horrifying thought, and one that fit in far too well with the fears Maya had about her sister. If she didn't solve this, if the killer truly *could* get away with this, then there really would be a woman's death on her hands.

Maya looked out over the lake, seeing the moon reflected on the water there. A waxing moon, not a full moon, so if he was trying to copy the moonlight killer, he was getting that part wrong.

Except…

Maya kept staring out over the water, looking at the reflection of the moon. The full moon wasn't the moon's only phase, and the moonstones certainly seemed to imply a link. Why leave something like that behind if the moon wasn't significant in all of this somehow?

Maya got out her phone, checking the dates of the other murders. It didn't take long to reference those dates against the phases of the moon. There had been one on the full moon, one when it was half full, one when it was gibbous, and now this murder, on the waxing moon.

Maya knew that she was on to something. She had to be. There was no way that this was all just some kind of coincidence.

Maya ran back towards the crime scene, not caring if the reporters there saw her. She ducked back under the crime scene tape then ran on until she found Marco down by the side of the club, looking around, obviously searching for any evidence that the CSI unit might not have found yet.

"What is it, Maya?" Marco said as he turned to her. His expression changed, obviously seeing how excited she was. "You've found something, haven't you?"

"It's the phases of the moon, Marco. He's killing according to the phases of the moon."

CHAPTER EIGHTEEN

"There has to be something," Maya said. "The moon has to mean something in all of this."

Maya found herself obsessing over the moon. She sat in a borrowed office in the Lagoon City PD and stared at her laptop, trying to work out how the moon was involved. There was an evidence board on the wall, a thick stack of files in the corner and a view out over the lakes that even in the daylight only served to remind Maya of the moonlight glinting off the water.

The moon and its phases were the key to this, she was sure of it. She just couldn't see how.

There was a lot of obvious symbolism that she already knew, because when she'd spent weeks chasing the Moonlight Killer it was impossible not to. The moon was associated with madness, and the belief that mental states were affected by its phases. It was associated with magic, this strange otherness in the sky that promised something unearthly to those obsessed with it. In a place with so much water, it was connected to any tidal flow the lakes possessed. It was traditionally a feminine symbol, and also a symbol of rebirth.

The problem wasn't finding potential answers but that such answers were too easy to find. There were a dozen symbolic meanings that might fit this situation, any or none of which might mean something to the killer. Narrowing that down felt next to impossible.

Marco set down a coffee beside Maya. Given how little sleep she'd gotten last night, she needed it. "I have the crime scene reports here now."

"Is there anything there that we don't already know?" Maya asked.

Marco shook his head. "The CSI team didn't find usable DNA or prints. The ligature is a standard type of rope. Really, the only thing we have that stands out is the moonstone."

"And I can't find the answers we need with that," Maya said. She couldn't keep the frustration she felt out of her voice.

"Maya, you've been focused on that one thing for so long now that I'm not sure you'd see the answer even if it were right there in front of you," Marco said. "Maybe take a break from that one thing. You could do some research on Laney Jackson, or something."

Maya thought about it, but the problem was simple. “I don’t think the connections between the victims are what matters here. I don’t know if we’re going to find the killer in their lives. I think that he’s just picking them out because they fit a type. Young, female, out at night, on the verge of changing something about their lives.”

“That’s the Moonlight Killer’s victim type,” Marco pointed out. “We need to find out what’s unique about *this* killer.”

That was easy to say, but as far as Maya could see, the only unique thing was the presence of the moonstones.

Or was that what she was meant to think?

“Do you ever get the feeling that the Moonlight Killer is just sitting back, watching us follow this trail of breadcrumbs that he knows we’ll find, laughing at us all the while because he knows the answers?” Maya asked Marco.

“You think he knows who all the killers are?” Marco didn’t look as though he thought that was likely.

“He’s given us clues in the past,” Maya pointed out. “He was obviously further along than we were.”

“That doesn’t mean that he’s done the work on the ground to discover every last detail,” Marco said. “If he knew everything, then why wouldn’t he just go out and take care of these guys himself? That seems like the kind of thing he’d do.”

It was the kind of thing he *had* done, before now. He’d gotten to prisoners, the ones who had most obviously been copying him, and he’d killed them. It had been just another demonstration of how resourceful and dangerous he was.

It was one more reason why Maya felt like a puppet, being jerked this way and that by a hidden puppeteer.

Maya decided to give Marco’s suggestion a try by focusing on Laney Jackson for a little while. Samit had already pulled what he could of her social media for Maya to go through, so Maya started there. Most of it just looked normal, although she noted the way pianos and snippets of Laney playing had started to appear over the course of the last few months. It was obvious that she’d been building up to her big debut for some time.

Was this where the killer had spotted her? Maya had seen cases before where killers had picked out their victims online, but there had also been more where they’d come across them in real life and gone from there. Still, Maya wasn’t going to let go of the possibility that the killer might have seen her online, or even been in contact, so she started to look through Laney Jackson’s emails and messages, trying to find any hint of someone who might have wanted to hurt her. People often weren't subtle about letting their feelings be known in such environments, so there was a good chance that if the killer had reached out to Laney before he killed her, it wouldn't be hard to spot.

Maya was still looking when a call came through to her phone. Maya was surprised to find that it was Agent Swift calling. A part of her suspected that it might be better to simply ignore the call, but that wasn't really an option. When the head of another taskforce was calling her, it was probably something that mattered.

At the same time, though, when that taskforce was dedicated to finding the Moonlight Killer, Maya could only worry.

"Agent Swift," she said, picking up and trying to keep that worry out of her voice. "What can I do for you?"

"You can tell me about the case you're currently working," Agent Swift said, straight to the point as usual. She didn't sound at all happy about it. "Because the last I heard, it was one for my department."

Maya felt a brief surge of relief at that, rather than the annoyance she would have usually felt. A part of her had been worrying that Agent Swift was calling because she'd worked out the link that the postcards had to the Moonlight Killer. This was just some of the same jurisdictional nonsense that Maya had been putting up with for a while now.

"This isn't the Moonlight Killer," Maya assured Agent Swift. "It's a similar killer, one using most of the same MO, but this one doesn't always kill on the full moon and he leaves a single moonstone behind at the scene."

"So a copycat?" Agent Swift asked.

"Possibly." Maya was willing to concede that much, but didn't want to give Agent Swift too much ground. There was a possibility that she might even try to lay claim to a copycat, pushing Maya out of the case that she needed to solve. "But I'm also working on the theory that the killer is coming at this from a different angle. Something to do with the moonstones."

"Ah, so we don't have a potential conflict between our taskforces," Agent Swift said. Maya couldn't tell if the more senior agent was disappointed by that or not. "I'll leave you to get on with your case."

Maya knew that she ought to just let the other agent go and be grateful that she wasn't going to interfere in Maya's case, but she couldn't resist the chance to find out more about a case that only Agent Swift could help her with.

"Agent Swift, I saw that your team has picked up a case in the last few days: the murder of Cassandra Moore?"

"That's right." Agent Swift sounded a little surprised that Maya was asking about the case.

"Are there any details that stand out from that one?" Maya asked. She was fishing for information, and doing it clumsily, but this was probably her best chance to get the answers she needed. If she didn't try, then she might never find out everything she needed to locate her sister.

"Why are you asking?" Agent Swift asked. "This is a Moonlight Killer case."

"Are you sure?" Maya asked. "Maybe you could send me over the file to review just in case?"

"Why do you want that?" Agent Swift asked. Now she sounded suspicious, rather than just puzzled.

Maya realized that she was pushing too hard. The information on the dead PI might prove useful in finding the man who had kidnapped her sister, but asking for it like this only increased the chance of Agent Swift realizing the link between the Moonlight Killer and the cases Maya was working. Maya needed to find a way to backtrack.

"I'm just trying to establish that my guy is limited to one city," Maya said. "With the kill taking place so close to one that's happened here, I thought there might be a link."

"We haven't found any moonstones here," Agent Swift said, as if that settled it. "They're separate cases, Agent Gray. Sending you the file would only confuse things. Sorry to have wasted your time."

Agent Swift hung up and Maya sighed with relief that she'd gotten away with that, even as she felt the frustration of not being able to get closer to answers. She felt a rush of fear too because she realized that she'd been talking about it on a line the Moonlight Killer might well be monitoring. Would he be angry that she'd tried to find out more about his last kill?

Maya shook her head, trying to clear it. She needed to focus on the case in front of her. She went back to Laney Jackson's emails, and that was when she froze, staring, barely able to believe what she could see there.

"Marco, there's an email here from Nils Schafer," Maya said.

"What does he want?"

"No, I mean that there's one in Laney Jackson's inbox. He had contact with her, even knew her. It's about the purchase of a couple of gemstones so that she could have them set into earrings. He signs off by saying that he hopes the preparations for her big debut are going well. He *knew* her, Marco. Well enough to know about the piano. Well enough to know about the debut."

That was a huge connection. It took someone who had only been a witness in Maya's mind and turned him into a potential suspect. It made a kind of sense, didn't it? This was a man who could source as many moonstones as he needed, and who wouldn't leave the kind of trail doing it that others might. If he siphoned off a few stones from each shipment he got, he could build up more than enough stock to see him through a whole murder spree.

"One connection could be a coincidence," Marco pointed out. He obviously didn't want Maya throwing all her efforts at this without more.

"So we need to find out if there are any other connections," Maya said. "Look into Nils Schafer. Have Samit go through whatever he can find of the man's online presence."

Maya started to look for connections from the opposite direction, starting to go through the social media accounts of the other victims, poring over pictures, searching through message strings for any mention of Schafer by name, or even of a gem merchant.

The searches quickly proved to be a dead end, leaving Maya with going through photographs one at a time, trying to find anything that might serve as a suitable link.

"Maya," Marco said. "I think I've got something. Heather Sullivan sometimes worked in catering. Well, look…"

He turned his phone to her. On it was a picture, obviously taken from Schafer's company website. It featured him at a formal dinner somewhere, standing next to a bunch of important looking people. Maya's attention was more on the back of the picture. Heather Sullivan stood there, waiting on tables.

Now, it seemed like too much of a coincidence to ignore. Schafer had a moonstone connection, and he also had clear connections to at least two of the victims, however brief. If he was the killer, then his business gave him an opportunity to meet potential victims.

Perhaps the moonstones weren't even really about the moon. Perhaps they were some kind of reference to his business, or to some obsession with gems.

Maya didn't know, but she *did* know that she and Marco needed to go talk to Nils Schafer again, this time as a suspect.

CHAPTER NINETEEN

The man they called Frank was watching from his control center at the heart of his bunker. He was always watching, or at least, those he employed to be his eyes and ears were. His own attention had to stray from time to time, either to deal with important matters or to maintain the pretense to the outside world that he was one of them, no different than his neighbors, if a touch more reclusive.

He *wasn't* like them, of course. He was so much more than most people, so much better, that it was almost painful watching them stumble through their lives. He saw them trying to become more, pretending that they could change into something new and special, and the need to take that from them was simply too strong.

For now, he was watching footage of Maya. Some of it consisted of snippets of press footage, strung together to give him every angle of her running around the latest crime scene as if she'd just found the answer to everything. Some of it was more discrete footage taken by a new employee, a paid set of eyes and ears.

Thoughts of *that* brought him back to thoughts of Cassandra. It wasn't a surprise to him that the FBI had identified her as his work. It wasn't even a surprise that Maya was looking into that case, or trying to, but still, it was an annoyance that would have to lead to some kind of reckoning. Only the fact that her colleague Agent Swift wasn't willing to give her what she wanted prevented Frank from reacting with violence towards one of his bunnies to teach Maya a lesson.

No, he would have to teach her a different way. He found himself staring at Maya in her interactions with Detective Spinelli, thinking about the last thing Cassandra had told him before she died. That they were a couple, that they were romantically involved. There was certainly a closeness there between them that he didn't like as he watched the pair of them. Maybe he could exploit that.

Now wasn't the moment, though. Now, Frank wanted to spend some time with his bunnies. He wanted to remind himself that there was a point to all of this, and that going to such trouble to keep them here was worth it.

It was important to remind himself of that because there had been so many frustrations along the way with this project that there were moments when he was tempted to finish the whole thing, take the gains that he'd made so far, kill the remaining bunnies, and just disappear into the ether. He knew that would hurt Maya and there was a certain satisfaction to that, but he also knew that if he did that, all that he had done so far would be for nothing.

He'd planned all of this and he would stick to the plan, even if it was difficult.

Frank slid on his mask and gloves, making sure that he had his taser and his knife. It was important not to take any chances while he was out there in the bunker. With his tools in place he went out there, enjoying the way that his bunnies scattered ahead of him.

Today, Frank was only interested in one of them, in the one who stood out from the rest of them, in Megan. She was special because of who her sister was. She *wasn't* her sister, wasn't dear Maya, with whom Frank shared such a special sense of closeness, but she was an adequate substitute for now.

Frank took his seat at the heart of his small kingdom and spoke, loud enough to be heard around the bunker.

"Megan. Oh, Megan! Come here little bunny."

She came forward, out of the shadows. It wasn't as if she had a choice about it, but it amused Frank to act as if she did. He gestured to the floor by his feet.

"Won't you join me, Megan? I have a story to tell you."

She came forward and stood there for a moment or two, but Frank fixed her with a cold stare.

"Sit down, Megan, or we can't begin our story."

She held on a moment longer, then sat down on the floor. That was good because Frank wasn't going to allow her to defy him for long.

"Now, I thought today that I would tell you the story of a man, a killer. One who likes to strangle his victims. One who does it underneath the moon, needing it shining there above him as he does his work."

Frank couldn't keep a note of contempt out of his voice at that. This man had copied him so much, yet managed to get the essence of it so badly wrong, that it was almost funny.

"The Moonlight Killer," Megan guessed. She didn't know who he was in that respect at least. She knew he was a killer, but not which, even now.

"No," Frank snapped back. "A lesser light. One whose work had been assumed to be that of another for months now. This lesser light likes to leave fragments of moonstone by his victims, calling cards, necessary elements of his process."

"Why are you telling me this?" Megan asked him.

"Because that is the man your sister is chasing this time," Frank said. "In her usual oh so energetic way. There was a time when I thought of dear Maya as almost an intellectual equal. Now, though…"

"She keeps solving these cases of yours," Megan pointed out. "She keeps winning your game."

Frank smiled to himself behind his mask. "True. Although for now, she is still blundering around blindly. She doesn't understand the significance of the moonstone to this man, doesn't understand what he is trying to achieve."

"And you do?" Megan asked him.

Frank nodded. For him, with the information he was able to get, the way he was able to piece things together, it was a simple matter to understand what was going on. He even had a fair idea, in this case, of who the guilty party was.

"I know who your sister is looking for, yes," Frank said.

"So why don't *you* catch him?" Megan asked. "Or kill him? If you know who he is, why have my sister do all of this?"

Frank shrugged. "Partly because the game is amusing. Having your sister at my beck and call pleases me. Partly because I only kill when I choose. Mostly though because I want the world to know the truth."

"What truth?" Megan asked.

Frank shook his head, not answering. If she couldn't see it, he wouldn't tell her. It became clearer with every killer Maya brought to justice, publicly eliminating deaths that weren't down to him, making it clear to the world in a way he never could have. Little by little, the noise fell away, and the pattern of his great work was revealed.

Soon, he was sure even dear Maya would see it. Perhaps that would be the moment to end this with *her* death. Not now, though. For now, she still had a killer to catch for him.

CHAPTER TWENTY

Marco drove as they headed back to Nils Schafer's house. He was a little worried about Maya as he did so. He knew that she was on edge. She obviously hadn't gotten much sleep last night thanks to the murder. He hadn't either, but it wasn't *his* sister whose life was at stake if they didn't manage to solve this case in time.

She was looking at her laptop as they drove, looking at something Samit had sent over on Nils Schafer.

"The closer we look at his business, the worse it looks," Maya said. "Everything here looks so shady."

"But does that make him a serial killer?" Marco asked. That was the key question for him. "Aren't we dealing with some sick guy with a strange compulsion to kill? Shady business practices don't matter for that."

"Maybe it's what he wants us to think," Maya suggested. "We've seen cases where people have covered up their crimes before by pretending that they're the Moonlight Killer. Maybe this is something to do with his business, maybe these women found out about the illegal parts, and he's just trying to make it look like the work of a serial killer to throw off the scent. Only then, why leave the moonstones?"

It was still possible. It was also possible that Schafer had simply been driven mad by whatever obsession with gems made him trade in them, or that whatever psychopathic tendencies drove him to kill also meant that he didn't care about the rules when it came to his business. They would need to ask him to find out.

Thankfully, they were almost at his lakefront house. Marco pulled up in front of it and Maya was already leaping out as the car came to a halt. He followed her to the door, where she was buzzing the intercom.

There was no answer at first, but Maya kept her finger on the buzzer. Marco knew she wasn't going to give up that easily.

Eventually, the door opened, revealing a woman who might have been some kind of member of Schafer's staff.

"We need to speak to Nils Schafer," Maya said, holding up her badge. "Now."

"I'm afraid Mr. Schafer isn't here," the woman said. "I'm just cleaning up the house while he's away."

Marco picked up on that. “Away? He’s going somewhere?”

The woman flinched slightly, as if aware that she’d just said the wrong thing. “I really don’t think I should-”

“Where is he?” Marco asked. “This is an FBI investigation. Do you want to make yourself into a potential accomplice by trying to hide him?”

Marco knew from his time in Cleveland when to apply pressure and when not to. Right now, if Schafer wasn’t here, that might mean that he was running.

“I… I think he’s on his way to the airport,” the woman said. “He asked me to call to get his private jet ready.”

A private jet. Schafer was running.

Maya obviously felt the same way. “We need to get to him before he reaches the airport.”

She ran for the car and Marco ran with her. He leapt into the driver’s seat and threw the car into motion.

“Get me directions for the airport,” he said.

“On it,” Maya replied, staring at her phone. “Left here.”

Marco took the car around the corner in a skid, hitting the gas again. He sped forward as fast as he dared. He’d done pursuit driving courses in the Cleveland PD and he used every moment of that training now, weaving through the traffic in the way without slowing down. His beaten up Explorer, Betsy, ate up the road, while he hit the sirens and lights to move the cars in front out of the way.

“Now right,” Maya said.

Marco could see signs for the airport now. He followed them, not slowing down. He could see the airport in the distance, along with a line of traffic obviously trying to get into the main part of it. Marco guessed that wouldn’t be where he and Maya were heading, even as they shot down past the cars there, ignoring the blaring horns that sounded around them.

Marco saw a side road with a sign saying, “private aircraft access only,” and threw the car into a tight turn. He could feel the Explorer fighting him with the effort of it, but he held that turn, determined not to lose even a second when Schafer might already be making preparations to get into the air.

“There!” Maya said, pointing.

Marco saw it too: a very familiar looking BMW, one that he’d seen before outside Schafer’s house. Their suspect was ahead, currently stationary at a barrier, talking to a security guard. Beyond the barrier was an open stretch of airfield, a couple of hangars, and a jet waiting next to a section of runway.

Marco didn't slow down; he couldn't if they were going to catch up to Schafer. Instead, he sped forward, trying to get to the barrier before Schafer got through it. The barrier rose, though, and Schafer must have seen them because now, his car sped forward.

Marco didn't stop for the security checkpoint, didn't even slow down as he shot onto the airfield in pursuit.

The BMW was fast, but Marco had modified Betsy plenty over the years, and the Explorer kept up easily, even closing the distance. A moment later and Maya wasn't sure if that was a good thing, because Schafer's bodyguard leaned out of the window, a gun in his hand.

"Down!" Maya yelled as the bodyguard started to fire.

Marco saw her draw her weapon and fire back, but with the movement of the car, even she seemed to have a hard time hitting anything.

Schafer zigzagged now, his bodyguard still firing, heading over in the direction of the hangars, obviously trying to lose them there. Marco kept pace with him, speeding along a section of air strip, ignoring the way it made his car bounce around.

A small plane heading straight at them as it taxied towards the runway was harder to ignore. Schafer's car sped around it, but Marco could see that by the time they reached it, there wouldn't be enough space to do the same.

"Marco, go left!" Maya yelled.

Marco did it instinctively, trusting that she'd seen something he hadn't. He had no time to ask what, though, only to pull hard on the wheel, sending the car into a skid that barely held. Marco realized that the skid had them heading straight into one of the hangars, and for a moment he found himself wondering if he should have done what Maya suggested after all.

Then he saw what Maya had seen: that the far side of the hangar was open. She'd spotted a shortcut. The Explorer shot through the empty space of the hangar, quickly coming out the far side. Marco headed off on a route parallel to the one he knew Schafer had to be taking to get to the private jet. Marco kept his eyes peeled for the BMW.

He spotted it between two of the buildings there and headed straight for it. The private jet was just ahead. If Schafer got to it, then it might be too late to stop him from escaping.

Marco floored the gas pedal, closing the distance. He was right behind Schafer's car now, but he needed to find a way to stop it.

Marco swung his Explorer into the left rear corner of the BMW, aiming for a classic PIT maneuver. He felt the moment of impact and a second later, the BMW was spinning, skidding to a halt in front of the private jet.

Maya jumped out as the Explorer drew to a halt, her weapon already up. Marco joined her, with his own weapon raised, ready to fire on the bodyguard.

He seemed to get the message, throwing his gun out of the window. He and Schafer got out of the car unsteadily, their hands raised.

"What's wrong, Schafer?" Maya demanded. "Running before we could find out that you're the one who killed those women?"

"What?" Schafer said. He looked incredulous and annoyed. "*That's* what you think is going on?"

"You sent us after one of your random clients to get rid of us so you would have time to escape," Maya said. "You have connections to at least two of the dead women."

"What connections?" Schafer demanded.

"Laney Jackson was one of your clients," Maya snapped back.

"She's dead?" Schafer looked, if anything, even more shocked. The expression looked far too genuine to Marco. "When?"

"Last night," Marco said. "Down by a local bar in town."

"But I wasn't even in town last night," Schafer said. "I was…"

"Yes?" Maya said.

Schafer shook his head.

"If you don't say anything, we're taking you in for murder," Marco pointed out. "Both of you."

Schafer shook his head again, but his bodyguard wasn't so sanguine about it.

"We were a town over, at a bar, meeting one of the boss's contacts. There will be witnesses, security footage. Plenty of people saw us."

"About what?" Maya demanded. She obviously wanted it to be a lie.

"Check the car," the bodyguard said. "Check the trunk."

"Marco?" Maya said. "You go. I'll cover them."

Marco went around to the trunk, popping it open. There was a briefcase within. The impact of the controlled collision had knocked it open, spilling its contents all over the trunk. A mixture of cut and uncut diamonds shone against the dark interior.

“Diamonds,” Marco said. He looked over to the bodyguard. “Where did these come from? Give me answers if you don’t want to go down with him.”

“Some of them are stolen,” the bodyguard said. “Some of them are smuggled. Conflict diamonds. I know all the details. I’ll tell you if you cut me a deal.”

Marco saw the fury on Schafer’s face as his bodyguard started to rat him out. That only encouraged Marco to go along with it.

Marco nodded. It was probably going to be the quickest way to wrap up everything that Schafer was involved in. The only problem was what he *wasn’t* guilty of. If he’d really been with a smuggler last night, over in a different town, then there was no way that he’d been the one to kill Laney Jackson or the other woman.

They’d hit a dead end.

CHAPTER TWENTY ONE

Maya sat in the Lagoon City PD, utterly frustrated. Her hands hovered over the keyboard of her laptop, but she had no idea what to type, no idea what might let her and Marco make progress in the case.

It didn't help that Detective Keymer was far too happy about them bringing in Nils Schafer and his bodyguard.

"You brought down a diamond smuggling operation without even trying to," the detective said. "You should be happier than this! We should be celebrating."

As far as Maya could see, there wasn't much to celebrate. Yes, they'd brought in a middleman in an operation to fence stolen and smuggled diamonds, but that only meant that they'd spent the morning chasing after a lead that wasn't related to their main case. They were slowly running out of time and Maya was no closer to an answer.

"If you want to work that side of things, be my guest," Maya said. She had no interest in trying to run down the rest of the diamond smuggling ring, not now. "My guess is that the bodyguard will give you everything you need if you cut him a deal."

The main thing she wanted right then was to get the detective to focus on that interrogation so that she could return her attention to trying to find answers in this case. Detective Keymer nodded and left, obviously thinking about what a big deal it would be to take down the whole network around the diamonds.

"You're going to let him have all the credit on the diamonds?" Marco asked.

Maya shrugged. "That doesn't matter. The man holding Megan isn't going to give us anything extra for catching diamond smugglers."

That was the only part of this that mattered: could she keep her sister safe, or not? The Moonlight Killer still had Megan in his hands and was still ready to kill her if Maya failed here.

She couldn't fail.

Maya threw herself back into the files, going over the information about the murders, trying to find links. She'd thought back at the scene of Laney Jackson's murder that the killer was killing according to the phases of the moon. Did that get her anywhere, though? Was there anything about it that could lead her back to the killer?

Maya found herself staring at charts of the moon's phases, trying to find some meaning in them. The trouble was that there was too *much* meaning. The moon had been a source of symbolism and myth pretty much since the dawn of time. Picking one element out of all of that seemed nearly impossible.

Maya was still trying when her phone rang. The moment she saw Agent Harris's name, Maya knew it wasn't going to be good. She might nominally be separate from her boss's control now that she was the head of her own taskforce, but that wouldn't stop Harris from causing problems here.

Maya still had to pick up, though.

"Sir?"

"Agent Gray, I've just been watching the news. Do you know what I saw there?"

"No, sir."

"I saw footage of you and Detective Spinelli crashing through the security at an airport, getting into a gun battle and endangering lives. *That's* what I saw."

Maya could feel her levels of annoyance rising. The whole point of her taskforce was that she didn't have to answer to Harris over the way she conducted this case, but it seemed to her that he was determined to find an excuse to bring her back under his control. He wanted to run things his way.

Maya couldn't allow that. His way consisted of focusing on the hunt for the kidnapper to the exclusion of everything else, against the rules the Moonlight Killer had set out in his "game." Trying to capture him again and again had only gotten people hurt and put the women he held in greater danger.

"We were in pursuit of a suspect," Maya said. "One who was attempting to make a run for it. If he'd made it to his plane, then he could have been in a non-extradition country by now and we would never have seen him again."

"Does that mean that you've caught the killer in this case?" Harris asked. "When can we expect you back here? I want to discuss your taskforce and some of its actions."

"The suspect turned out not to be the killer," Maya said.

Maya heard the pause on the other end of the line.

"You chased and shot at an innocent man?" Harris said, the anger and disbelief in his voice coming through all at once.

"He was a *long* way from innocent," Maya assured her boss. "He's implicated in a major criminal enterprise; he's just not the killer."

That seemed to mollify Harris a little, but only a little. "I still want to talk when you get back, Gray. I'm not happy with the way you're running your taskforce."

Maya knew that she had to stand up for her team then, or Harris would try to fold it back into his department again. He'd been trying to do that almost since she forced him to give her the taskforce to avoid any more debacles as the Moonlight Killer outsmarted Harris.

"With respect, sir, it's *my* taskforce, and the way I'm running it has resulted in the capture of half a dozen killers, the release of several of the hostage taker's captives, and a lot of progress on *this* case."

It was as close as Maya could come to telling Harris to butt out without risking losing her job. She could tell immediately that Harris wasn't happy about it.

"You'd better hope that you succeed in this one too," Harris said. "The first time your methods get a woman killed, you're off this case."

He hung up abruptly, leaving Maya to stew in her anger. If a woman died, then being taken off the case would be the least of her worries. That woman might be her sister. Even if it wasn't, then with Harris back in charge of things, Megan would be in more danger.

It meant that it was more important than ever that Maya found answers in this case and there simply didn't seem to *be* answers. Maya couldn't accept that, she wouldn't. She started to work through the information she had on the victims again, trying to find anything that might hint at who had targeted them, rather than someone else.

The trouble was that she already had answers there, too. Maya could *see* that these were women who were on the verge of starting something new, just as she could see that the killer had targeted women who were likely to be out at night, but just knowing that wasn't enough. It didn't get her to answers. Understanding the general pattern wasn't enough; she needed specific evidence that linked back to the killer.

"What was all that with Harris?" Marco asked. He looked worried when Maya glanced up.

"Not now," Maya said. The last thing she wanted was to talk about Harris when she was trying to focus on the case.

"Maya-"

"Not *now,* Marco. I'm trying to focus on these files."

Marco didn't give up, though. "I know. That's why I'm asking. I've seen you obsess before, Maya. This is what it looks like. You've barely slept and now you're staring at the files like if you only bang your head against this brick wall long enough it will give way. I'm worried about you."

"It's not me you need to worry about," Maya said. "It's whoever will die if we don't solve this."

"Maya…" Marco reached out for her then, but Maya got up and moved back. She hadn't intended to turn this into an argument, but the frustrations were building up inside her so much that she couldn't help it.

"I don't need you to be a boyfriend right now, or whatever you are." They hadn't exactly clarified that yet. "I need you to be a partner. I need to focus on the case. I need…" Maya could hear that she'd started to raise her voice. "I need to go get some air."

She left the office, not giving Marco any time to answer, heading out into the open air of the city. She knew as she walked that she was acting out of frustration and anger. She also knew that Marco was just trying to help. Just knowing those things didn't make it easier.

A part of her wanted to go back to him, kiss him as an apology, briefly melt into his arms and try to make things up to him for snapping at him, but that wasn't the FBI agent in her speaking. That was the Maya who had gone on dates with him, who couldn't help being attracted to him every time she was together with him. As an agent, she needed some time alone. She needed to be able to think.

Maya walked the streets of the city. It really did seem as if everywhere had a view out over one of the lakes and Maya found herself heading towards one of them as she walked, trying to relax enough to just think for once. That was the problem with her whole situation: the more she tried to force answers, the less likely they were to come to her, but with such a short deadline, and with so much on the line, it was impossible not to.

Maya couldn't stop thinking about the moonstones as she walked. They were the one unique element of the case, which meant that they had to be at least a part of the way into all of this. The question was how.

Maya knew more about moonstones than she had at the start of all of this. She knew about their physical properties, about the scarcity of the clearest blue ones. She knew more about the gem dealers who traded in them. What else was there to learn? Maya felt sure that if she could unravel more of what the moonstones meant to the killer, that would help her to get deeper into his mind. Right now, that was the only way that she was going to narrow down the kind of man it was likely to be.

Maya was still trying to think about all of that and where the moon might fit into all of this when she saw the New Age store.

Its window display featured everything from Tibetan mandalas to elaborate statuettes. Signs in the window promised healing treatments that seemed to mingle traditions in alternative therapies without hesitation, promising everything from acupuncture to electrostimulation therapy.

Maya's eye, though, was drawn by a display of jewelry in the window, pendants and rings, brooches and occasionally just stones. There were small signs next to some of them proclaiming their healing properties.

In that moment, she found herself thinking about the moonstones differently. Before, she'd been thinking about them in their role as gemstones, or for their connection to the moon. Now, she found herself thinking about what mystical or health properties might be claimed for the moonstones. Was it possible that the killer was trying to achieve some kind of particular effect? Was he trying to change something in himself, or his victims?

Maya didn't know, but she wanted to find out more. Maybe if she learned about moonstones and whether they fit into all of this, then she would understand enough about the killer and his motivations to finally start to close in on him.

Maya paused at the door, wondering whether she should call Marco and get him to come down here. No, not yet. She needed to know if there was more to this before she called him, and she didn't want to have to apologize to him for snapping at him either.

Taking a breath, Maya plunged into the interior of the store.

CHAPTER TWENTY TWO

The interior of the store smelled to Maya of jasmine and incense, pleasant but with a slight burnt note behind it that she didn't like as much. The shop looked as though it had been arranged through the time honored method of just piling up as much stuff as possible wherever it would fit, so that bookshelves on one wall were partly obscured by racks of clothing, which intruded upon displays of what were marked as healing crystals and chimes. Soft flute music played in the background.

The assistant there was a woman in her forties, wearing a multicolored knitted shawl over a long white dress with work boots sticking out from underneath. She had a headscarf holding back a tangle of dark hair and wore round glasses that seemed slightly too large for her slender features. She was currently in the middle of helping a customer make a selection from what looked like a display of scented candles, so Maya took the opportunity to head over to the bookshelves and look for anything that might mention moonstones.

She found books on birth signs and their attendant gemstones, but that didn't seem right. From what Maya recalled, the women who had been killed were all relatively different ages and had been born at different times of the year. It wasn't as simple as the moonstones being just their birth stones.

Maya suspected that the killer was thinking more in terms of whatever powers were ascribed to the stones. He obviously believed in such things and was trying to use those powers in some way. The questions were what way and why.

"Sorry to keep you waiting," the proprietor said, walking over, while a rattle of wind chimes announced the departure of the other customer. "What can I do for you?"

Maya took out her badge. "I'm Agent Gray, with the FBI. I was hoping you could help me."

"Me?" the store owner said, looking surprised by the possibility. "What can I do to help the FBI? If you're hoping I'm one of those psychics who tells you where to find all the answers, I'm afraid that's not the kind of thing I do."

Maya couldn't tell if she was joking or if she really thought that Maya might have gone in there to have a psychic provide the identity of the killer. All Maya could do was press on.

"Can I ask your name?" Maya said.

"Rosie," the proprietor said.

"Well, Rosie, I need to know about the significance of various types of gemstones. Particularly moonstones. Do you think you can help me out with that?"

Maya saw the other woman nod. "Yes, of course. I'd be happy to help. Is this... is this about the murder the other night? I saw the coverage on the news."

Maya nodded. She didn't say that it was about a whole series of murders, or reveal the exact role of the moonstones. So far, that seemed to have been left out of the media. Still, she was going to have to give those details to Rosie at some point in case they were significant.

"Do you stock moonstones?" Maya asked. It was still possible that she might stumble on someone who had sold the killer his.

Rosie shook her head though. "Not really. Maybe an occasional one in a piece of jewelry."

"But you understand how they fit into something like crystal healing?"

She saw the other woman nod. "Yes, up to a point."

"What can you tell me about moonstones?" Maya said. "Is there any reason that they might be significant to someone? To a killer?"

She saw Rosie hesitate. "I... moonstones have always been associated with the moon, and there's a traditional link to madness there. Their presence is said to be calming, helping people to focus. People also think that they help with accepting change and making a smoother transition to new beginnings."

Maya had speculated about some of that before, but here and now, it seemed far more relevant. Was it possible that a killer acting because of some kind of personality disorder knew how ill he was, and the moonstones were an attempt to change it? Was this someone's terrifying attempt to heal themselves?

There was another part that Maya picked up on as well. "They're linked to new beginnings?"

She saw Rosie nod. "Because of the shifting phases of the moon, traditionally, people would wear them at moments of great change as a reminder that change can help you to move on to something better, that change is a natural part of the cycle of life."

And the killer had been targeting women right on the cusp of change in their lives. Which meant that Maya might have to reveal everything. It was a lot to give away to someone not on the case, but if it could help her get an answer to all of this then it might be worth it.

"Could someone… I don't know, steal that change?" Maya asked. If the killer was conducting a ritual with women on the cusp of change, was it possible that he was trying to take advantage of that moment of change in some way for his own ends? Was it possible that he was trying to change something about himself?

Rosie looked puzzled. "What do you mean?"

Maya sighed. "Look, for this to make sense, I'm going to have to tell you details of an active investigation. Are you ok with that?"

Rosie seemed to think for a moment, then nodded.

Maya tried to set it out as simply as she could. "There have been multiple murders around the city over the last few months, all young women on the brink of some kind of change in their life. Moonstones were left at every scene."

She could see the look of horror in the other woman's eyes. She knew then that revealing the details had gone way past the proprietor's comfort zone.

"Rosie, can you help me with this?" Maya asked. "Is it possible that the killer thinks that he's somehow stealing the change that was about to happen in these young women's lives, trying to use it himself?"

"I don't know," Rosie said. She put a hand to her mouth. "A serial killer. There's a serial killer and no one told us. We all just thought…"

Maya didn't get to hear what she thought, given the way the other woman trailed off. Probably that it was the work of the Moonlight Killer, or just a series of isolated killings, each one barely reported in the local press.

"Rosie, focus," Maya said. "I'm working to catch the man who did this, but to do that, I need to know more about the way he might be thinking. Could he be trying to steal the change from these women's lives to use himself?"

"I… maybe?" Rosie said. "I guess, if he thought he was taking some part of their essence. I'm sorry, I don't really know. For something like this, you'd really have to talk to Guru Alexander up at the retreat."

"What retreat?" Maya asked.

Rosie led the way over to a notice board on one wall of the store. There were flyers there for everything from acupuncturists to yoga instructors, but Rosie was pointing at one in particular.

It advertised the Lakeview Healing and Self Perfection Retreat, run by a "Guru Alexander Olenik."

"The retreat is a big deal here," Rosie said. "People come from all over the state and beyond to stay there. They run breathwork and meditation classes, tai chi, different healing sessions…"

"And Guru Alexander would know about moonstones?" Maya asked. She didn't want to spend her time driving out of town if it wasn't going to get her any information she didn't already possess. She didn't have enough time left to waste any of it. A day and a half, that was all now.

"Crystal therapy is one of the retreat's specialties," Rosie said. "If anyone can tell you what you need to know, it will be Guru Alexander."

Maya hoped so. "Thank you. You've been very helpful."

Maya waited until she was out of the store and down the street before she started to look up the retreat on her phone. She still wanted a little more information before she committed to going over there. She wanted to see some evidence that they actually used moonstones there, or at least did the crystal therapy that the store owner had suggested they focused on.

It wasn't hard to find the Lakeside Retreat's website, which looked expensively crafted, with professional photographs taken of its facilities, designed to bring in the most expensive possible clientele. A quick glance through the retreat's list of facilities suggested that it boasted elegantly simple rooms, a fine dining restaurant, a couple of pools, a gym, several specialist meditation rooms, a sensory deprivation chamber, a sauna… It seemed like a strange combination of upmarket hotel, health spa, and monastery.

Maya found a page dedicated to the retreat's founder and owner: Guru Alexander. There was a picture there of a man in his forties, with dark hair down to his shoulders and a carefully trimmed beard. He was bare-chested and standing on one leg in a yoga pose, revealing a muscled physique adorned with beads and crystals. Crucially, Maya saw a pendant around his neck with a stone that looked far too familiar.

He was wearing a large moonstone.

A part of Maya wanted to rush there to speak to him immediately, but she wasn't about to do it without completing her research. Maya used her phone to check Olenik's name on the FBI database. When it came back with one conviction, twenty years ago, for violently attacking a woman, it was all Maya could do to keep from going there straight away to arrest him.

Maya forced herself to keep looking over the retreat's website instead, wanting to get as much information as possible before she went there. That she *would* go there now was certain; Maya just wanted to be ready when she did.

She was looking through a series of promotional photos when Maya saw something that stopped her short. She called Marco immediately. She needed him with her for this.

"Maya?"

"Marco, I…" She remembered the reason she was out there in the first place. "Look, I'm sorry I snapped at you before, but I think I've found something. Can you pick me up? I'm a couple of blocks over from the department."

"What's the rush?" Marco asked. "What did you find?"

As an answer, Maya sent over a screenshot of the photograph that had caught her attention so utterly. In it was Guru Alexander, the man who ran the retreat, the man who had been in prison for attacking a woman. He was wearing a long white robe and sat there with his legs crossed, leading some kind of meditation practice with the moonstone again plainly visible around his neck.

"What am I looking at?" Marco asked. "Some guy meditating?"

"That is Guru Alexander Olenik, an expert in alternative therapies who runs a retreat outside of town. A guy who is apparently an expert on harnessing the properties of crystals. A guy who wears a moonstone. A guy with a criminal record for attacking his ex-wife. But look past him, on the right. What do you see?"

Maya looked again too, wanting to be sure that she'd gotten it right. The image wasn't large, and it was possible that she'd been mistaken, but no, she was right. There, in the background, meditating a little behind the guru, was Reba Andrews.

"I'll be right there," Marco promised.

Maya hoped so. The sooner they got to the retreat the better. Its guru had a lot of questions to answer.

CHAPTER TWENTY THREE

Maya had to admit that the Lakeside Retreat was even more impressive in real life than it had been in the photographs. It was clear that no expense had been spared in building it, creating a broad campus of facilities that most hotels would have been envious of.

It was set among a few trees, which provided shelter from the rest of the world so that it might have been alone as it pressed up against the shore of the lake it was next to. Maya got the impression that the whole area around it had been carefully landscaped to create the impression of gently ordered serenity. The main building, meanwhile, was a curving creation of glass and steel, painted white, with banners around the side depicting what appeared to be symbolic phases of the moon.

"That can't be a coincidence, can it?" Maya said to Marco as they pulled up outside.

"I'm not sure I believe in coincidences," he replied. "At least not in ones that big."

Nor did Maya. The killings had to be linked to this place, and Guru Alexander seemed like exactly the person to ask about it. Maya headed inside, into a large reception area whose floor appeared to be one giant mandala design, and around which plenty of plants had been set to create nooks and alcoves. Some held mats on which people were meditating, while others held chairs and small tables, where people were reading or drinking tea. A modern white reception desk that looked more extruded than built dominated the space in front of a staircase leading up to the rest of the facility.

The young woman behind that desk was blonde-haired and toned, probably in her mid-twenties, dressed in all white sports gear, looking more like a personal trainer than a receptionist.

"Welcome to the Lakeside Retreat," she said in a bubbly tone. "How can I help you today?"

"We'd like to speak to Guru Alexander," Maya said.

The receptionist smiled back at her, but it was an apologetic smile.

"I'm sorry, but as you can probably understand, the guru is very much in demand. He's leading a session right now, and private consultations have to be booked in advance."

Maya realized that the receptionist thought that she and Marco were there looking for some kind of treatment. Maya quickly got her badge out, setting it down on the desk with a precise click.

"We're not here for a consultation," Maya said. "We're in the middle of an investigation and we need to speak to Guru Alexander at once. Several women have been killed."

That got a look of shock from the receptionist. It was enough to crack her pleasant, helpful demeanor for a second.

"I… I guess if you come up with me, you could wait until his session's done?"

She obviously still didn't want to disturb the guru. Maya saw Marco nod.

"That's fine, we'll wait up there."

Maya couldn't tell if he was just agreeing with the receptionist or telling Maya that they should do it that way, reminding her not to go charging in. Maya was willing to go along with it, for now. It wouldn't be easy, though, because Maya was all too aware of the seconds ticking by until her deadline. Still, as long as Guru Alexander didn't try to run, she could force herself to wait. It would be easier to ask him questions as a suspect if he was cooperating.

She and Marco followed the receptionist up the stairs and along a couple of corridors, flanked by elegant suites of rooms. They finally came to a halt in a space in front of a large hall, where Guru Alexander seemed to be in the middle of leading a tai chi session, moving slowly and gracefully with a whole class full of others around him. It looked peaceful, the whole class looking serene as they moved in unison.

There were a few chairs set out in the corridor in front of the hall, obviously there to give people a space to wait for the next session. The receptionist gave Maya and Marco a worried look as she left them there, as if concerned that the two of them would burst in there the moment that she left.

For the moment, at least, Maya was content to wait, keeping her eyes on Guru Alexander, a part of her trying to spot any signs of the killer inside him. She knew it didn't work like that, though, so Maya paced the corridor instead.

"He'll be out soon enough," Marco said, obviously still trying to get her to be patient. "If we can interview him without it being hostile, he might give us more than if we head in there."

"I know, Marco," Maya said. He was still treating her as if she were too impulsive and unprofessional to be trusted. The worst part was that, far too often, he was right.

For now, Maya looked at some of the pictures hung up on the walls, trying to distract herself long enough to wait for the guru to finish. Some of them were inspirational quotes, while others appeared to be elegantly minimalist pen and ink depictions.

Maya found her eyes caught by some of the other pictures on the walls, showing smiling students in group pictures with Guru Alexander. Maya found herself scanning them, looking for Reba Andrews.

Maya was still looking when she found Dianne Smith staring back at her. Maya's eyes widened at that.

"Marco, look," she said, pointing.

Marco came over, staring for a second or two before he saw it. "Two of them were here?"

"Check the others," Maya said. She was already looking at the next photograph. It took her two more photographs to find the next of them, Laney Jackson staring out at her.

"I've got Heather Sullivan here," Marco said, looking at another of the pictures.

"They were here, Marco," Maya said. "They were all here."

This was the link between them. They'd all been visitors here, and they'd all been in Guru Alexander's classes. His, not anybody else's. This was a man who wore a moonstone, who was connected with the rituals used, and who had known all of the women. A man with a history of violence too. Maya wasn't prepared to wait any longer. There simply wasn't enough time.

Opening the door to the hall, Maya walked into the middle of the tai chi class.

People turned to stare at her as she did so. Maya held her badge out in front of her, as if that would push people back out of her way.

"Alexander Olenik, I'm with the FBI and you're under arrest," she said. She wasn't waiting for the guru to answer questions anymore. He could do that down at the local police department.

"Hey, you can't be in here!" a man in front of Maya said.

"Leave the guru alone," a woman added. They moved in front of Maya, blocking her path. Other members of the class moved in, so that in just a matter of seconds they were all around her.

In that moment, Maya was suddenly afraid. The people there might have looked peaceful while they were all doing tai chi together, but they looked a lot less serene now. A group of people might close in on her and drag her down, stopping her from ever getting close to their precious guru. If they decided to attack, so many of them might prove deadly even though they weren't armed. Maya found herself wondering if she needed to draw her gun.

The guru came forward through it all, still looking as serene as he had while doing tai chi.

"Friends, that's enough. Step back and give the FBI agent some room. Please, I won't have any violence here. Let the anger you feel flow away. Remember, the world only has the power to affect you that you give it."

He came to stand in front of Maya and Marco, his expression still not giving anything away.

"I will come peacefully," he said, holding his hands out for Maya to cuff him. "What's all this about?"

"Murder."

*

Maya sat across a table from Guru Alexander in the Lagoon City PD's interrogation suite, trying to get a read on him. It wasn't easy because he simply didn't seem to care that he was in there.

His lawyer did, though.

"You have no right to simply barge into the middle of my client's workplace and arrest him like that. What evidence do you even have?"

The lawyer was a man in his early thirties, sharp-suited and with an edge to him that suggested he was expensive. It seemed that the guru could afford the best. Maya's eye, though, was drawn to a small bracelet around the lawyer's wrist of what looked like healing crystals. Was this another of Guru Alexander's students?

"We have evidence that four women who are now dead were in Mr. Olenik's classes," Marco said.

"That's Guru Alexander," the lawyer shot back. Yes, definitely one of his students.

Guru Alexander put a hand on his lawyer's shoulder. "Dan, it's all right. Remember to stay centered. Agents, do you really think that I hurt any of these women?"

Maya cocked her head to the side. "You have a history of doing that kind of thing."

She saw the guru wince slightly at that, the first reaction from him that wasn't utterly serene.

"You mean my conviction? It was an evil thing for me to do. I don't deny that. But while I was in prison, I had an awakening. I started meditating, and somewhere in it, I found a moment of… clarity. I saw how it was possible to change, that the whole *world* is in a constant state of change. I embraced it. I also embraced pacifism."

"As you'd know if you'd read his books," the lawyer said. He sounded less like a lawyer now and more like a fan, an obsessed one at that.

The strange thing, though, was that Guru Alexander sounded as though he meant it. Maya had seen how he'd reacted back when she'd gone to arrest him. This was not a man who lashed out casually at women. Maybe he *had* changed.

She needed more than that, though.

"Where were you last night?" Maya asked.

"I was taking part in an all-night meditation exercise with some of my students," the guru replied. "I'm sure they would be happy to vouch for me."

So he had an alibi, but not much of one, given how devoted his followers seemed to be to him. Maya had no doubt that it would be easy for him to find ones who would lie for him if he needed it.

"You seem very calm about all of this, given the trouble you're in," Marco said.

Guru Alexander spread his hands. "I have every confidence that things will work out well. I have done nothing wrong here."

Maya decided to come at things from another angle. "Do you use moonstones in your practices?"

The guru nodded. "We do. They are an important symbol of transformation. You saw the banners outside our retreat? Each symbolizes a phase of the moon. A phase of the transformative process that we go through with those who join us."

Six phases. Maya found herself focusing on that, the moment stretching out for her.

"People like Reba Andrews, Heather Sullivan, Laney Jackson, and Dianne Smith?" Marco said.

"I do not know the names, but I teach many people."

"Those women were in your classes," Maya said. "They have also all turned up dead with moonstones on them."

The guru looked momentarily puzzled. "That would seem to suggest some kind of ritual of transformation, but to kill in it…"

"I don't think you should say any more, Guru Alexander," his lawyer said.

The guru shrugged. "A wise man knows when to take advice."

Maya looked over to Marco, then stepped out of the room with him. Detective Keymer was out there, looking excited.

"It's him. It's obviously him," the detective said. "He's had his weird little cult thing going for a while now. He gets people far too obsessed with him. I wouldn't be surprised if he tried to use his position to take advantage of these women or something, then killed them when they said no."

Maya's attention was on Marco. "What do you think?"

"I want to take another run at him. I'm not buying this whole serenity thing. What about you?"

"I'm… not sure," Maya said. "He has an alibi, after all."

"Not a good one."

"No," Maya agreed, "but it also occurs to me that even if the center is the link, that doesn't mean it has to be him doing the killing. Maybe a student or something?"

Detective Keymer didn't seem convinced. "Are you kidding? None of them there do anything without his say so. It's him."

"Maybe," Maya said. "Marco, if you want to go back in there, do it."

"What are you going to be doing in the meantime?" Marco asked.

"There's something he said. Something I want to check up on."

CHAPTER TWENTY FOUR

Back in the office she and Marco had borrowed, Maya sat staring at the retreat's website again, this time focusing on the description of its underlying philosophy and process. It was a section she hadn't paid attention to before because it hadn't seemed like the most relevant part for the case. Now, Maya found herself wondering if it was actually the most important thing of all.

Transformation mirrors the phases of the moon, although it is more chaotic. We start out so full, so sure of what we are. Then realization begins, and we become the merest sliver, a crescent. We grow, we become the waxing moon, but we must still work. We become the half-moon then and for a time we find balance, but balance is not enough, it is stagnation. So we continue to wax, becoming gibbous, almost full again. Our minds want to tell us that we have succeeded, but there is one more stage. We become the new moon, dark and silent, refreshed and peaceful.

Maya had said it to Marco, back on the shoreline where Laney Jackson had been killed: the killer was murdering his victims according to the phases of the moon. But it was more than that: he was working his way through the specific process of transformation advocated by the retreat.

He was trying to change something about himself, to become the new moon, empty and quiet, that Guru Alexander suggested was the endpoint of the process.

Was this a killer trying to stop himself from being a killer? Or was it someone so desperate to change some other aspect of their lives that they were willing to kill to achieve it? Maya wasn't sure if that made a difference; what mattered was the process that the killer had chosen, working his way through the steps in the most lethal way possible.

A six-step process suggested six victims. Did the killer still have two to go? Were two more women going to die if Maya didn't catch him? It was both worse and more immediate than that, of course. If Maya didn't come up with an answer by tomorrow at midnight, then she would fail in the Moonlight Killer's deadly game, and a woman's life would be forfeited. Maya couldn't allow that to happen.

She kept looking over the retreat's section about its process, then started to go over the case files for the four victims, trying to take in as much information as possible. Maya got the locations and started to plot them on a map, seeing if that would help. The first thing she noticed was that they seemed to line up, forming a line heading roughly southeast to northeast across the city, almost to its edges.

The second thing Maya saw was that there was a murder missing. Three of the kills were spaced neatly, one after another at regular intervals. One, Reba's, stood out from the others, with a gap to the next.

Maya went back to the retreat's site, then started to check the dates of the murders she knew about already against the phases of the moon. She'd done it before, but she wanted to be certain about it.

The results came back the same as last time: there had been murders on the full moon, the waxing moon, the half-moon, and the gibbous moon. There was no kill so far on the crescent moon.

That didn't fit the pattern. If the killer was working his way through the stages of the retreat's process, then he should have started with a full moon, then jumped to a crescent, before building up stage by stage to a gibbous moon.

Either he'd missed a step, which didn't seem likely to Maya, or somehow she'd missed a murder. Was it possible that one had slipped through the cracks in her hurry to get on with the investigation?

Maya started to check her earlier work on the local PD's casefiles. There weren't any kills mentioning jewelry that she'd missed, though. No moonstones that had been written off as just another brooch or pendant belonging to the victim. There was nothing there that hadn't been mentioned the first time.

Maybe it was better to go with the dates and work from that? Maya looked for any murders where a woman had been strangled in the months since Reba Andrews's murder, but before the death of Heather Sullivan, since the murder she was looking for would have to come between those two. Maya took the dates of the resulting files and checked them against the phases of the moon.

Only one had taken place on the night of a crescent moon, that of Bella Simonetti. Maya pulled up the file, reading the details, trying to get a sense of what had happened. It seemed that Bella had been found in an alleyway after an anonymous tip-off. She'd been strangled with a length of rope in a way that was consistent with the other murders, but again, no one seemed to have made the link between all of them. Either the police had assumed that they were all individual incidents or they simply hadn't wanted to admit the possibility that they had a home grown serial killer in their midst.

Maya read through the report, hoping for any mention of jewelry there that had been worded in such a way that a search wouldn't pick it up. Even though the date was consistent, without the moonstone to prove the connection, it was impossible to make a definitive link to the other murders. Maya needed that link if she was going to include it with the others and try to finish establishing the pattern that she'd started to build.

Maya looked through the case file until she found the name of the detective assigned to be the lead on the case: Detective Bauer. Maya got up from her seat, heading out into the bullpen of the department.

"I'm looking for Detective Bauer," she called out. "I need to talk with him about one of his cases."

"Bauer isn't in today," another detective supplied. "It's his day off."

"Is there a number I can call for him?" Maya asked.

The other detective shook his head. "You'll be lucky. If he's not on call, then knowing Tom, he's fishing. His phone will be off. He doesn't like scaring the fish."

Maya hesitated for only a second, thinking of Marco back in the interrogation room, still trying to get answers out of Guru Alexander. A part of her wanted his help on this, but if the guru *was* a part of this, then it was better if he kept going with the interrogation. They had to use their resources wisely when they only had a little time left.

"Ok," she said. "I need someone to show me where he goes fishing."

*

Maya pulled up by the lake, hoping that she'd followed the directions correctly. She'd come alone in a car borrowed from the Lagoon City PD's pool of them. She hadn't wanted to pull Marco from his interrogation of the guru. There was still a chance that Guru Alexander would prove to be their guy, and it seemed better to Maya for now if the two of them split up to cover as much ground as possible.

She hoped that this lead played out for her. If not, then it was just more time wasted when she had so little of it left. Getting out of the car, Maya scanned the lake, hoping that the detective would be there at the shore, able to talk to her.

All she saw by the shore was an old jetty with a few boats tied up there. Another boat sat out on the water, far enough out that it was hard to make out much about its occupant. He seemed to be fishing, though, so hopefully this was the detective she needed.

"Detective Bauer!" Maya called over the water.

If he glanced up, Maya didn't see it. She tried waving both her arms in his direction, trying to catch his attention. No, still no response. Maya looked over to the moored boats. She was just going to have to go out there to speak to him.

Maya went over to them. Most of the boats would have needed keys to start, but there was an old rowboat there, with oars tucked away under a tarp. Maya untied it from the jetty and set off in it, rowing smoothly, pulling across the surface of the lake in even strokes.

She got about halfway out there to the other boat when she realized that it was heading towards her now. Had Detective Bauer realized that she was there to talk to him? Maya turned and waved.

This close, Maya could make out more of the detective. He was a heavyset man in his fifties, dressed in casual clothes with a life preserver over the top. He also didn't look happy.

"Stop there!" he called out as he got closer. "What do you think you're doing, stealing someone's boat? You picked the wrong day for it, lady. I'm a cop."

"You're Detective Bauer," Maya said, pulling alongside him.

"How do you know that?"

"I'm Agent Gray, with the FBI. I came out here to speak with you. It's urgent. I need to know about the Bella Simonetti case."

"There's nothing urgent about that," Bauer said. "Simonetti has been dead for months. You're interrupting my day off."

"Her case might be linked to several others I'm looking into," Maya replied. "Ones where a moonstone was left at the scene."

The detective shrugged that off. "There was nothing like that at the crime scene. You're wasting your time and mine, Agent Gray."

Maybe, but Maya had to be sure.

"You're certain there's no way one could have been there?" she asked.

"I'm good at my job, Agent."

Perhaps, but he wasn't being very helpful now.

"Maybe one was there but someone took it before you got there," Maya suggested.

"Maybe, but I have no way of knowing that," Detective Bauer pointed out. He seemed to relent a little. "Besides, we got there quickly that day and there was no one around. The only person who could have taken anything from the scene was whoever called it in."

“Whoever?”

“An anonymous tip, made from a burner cell phone that had been paid for in cash so we couldn’t trace it to an individual.”

Maybe the local PD couldn’t, but if Maya was lucky, whoever had made the call might still have the phone.

“Is there a record of the number?” she asked.

“Sure,” the detective said. “It will be in the file.”

In that case, Maya needed to get back to shore and head back towards the city. She needed Samit to trace a cell phone for her.

CHAPTER TWENTY FIVE

"Left and then on for about another half-mile."

Maya followed Samit's directions as she drove, pushing through the streets of the city, trying to close in on the phone that he was tracking for her.

"How close can you get me to it?" Maya asked. That was a concern. If all he could do was trace the phone to a particular cell tower, then in a city that could mean any one of thousands of people.

"I can put you within a couple of yards," Samit said. "The local PD just tried checking the number for a name, rather than tracing the GPS signal from the phone. Keep going. It's not far. I'm monitoring your progress with GPS on *your* phone and with traffic cam footage."

That was impressive, if slightly creepy. It made Maya wonder exactly how closely the Moonlight Killer was monitoring her as she worked. She knew that he listened in to some of her calls, but did he know where she was at all times? Did he watch her through her phone's camera, or through local security cameras? The more Maya thought about it, the more worrying it was.

For now, though, she had to focus on getting to whoever had made the call. Was it the killer? Maya doubted it, but she still wanted an explanation. She'd seen a transcript of the call. A killer might have been more panicked, or calmly gloating, but this read more like someone knowing that he had to report the presence of a body, but not wanting to get involved.

Except that right now, he definitely was involved. Maya needed answers, and she hoped that the individual who had made the call could help to provide at least one.

"It should just be on your right," Samit said. "Pull over."

Maya did so and found herself opposite a big, run-down building that looked as though it had been abandoned some time ago. Maya watched it carefully, eyes going from window to window. She thought she saw a flicker of movement in there. It seemed that the place wasn't quite abandoned after all.

Maya moved in, keeping her call to Samit going as she tried the door to the place. The lock was broken, letting her swing it open easily. The interior was dusty and quite dirty, with graffiti on a couple of the walls nearby and piles of trash left near the door. It looked like the kind of place where nothing except rats would live, but this was where the phone signal was coming from.

"You're getting closer," the tech said. "It's definitely in that building. North corner. The elevation suggests you need to be up a level."

Taking Samit's advice, Maya found a staircase that would let her go upwards. It was rickety, as though it should have been pulled down years ago. Then again, the whole place looked like that.

Maya headed up, finding herself on a broad landing with doors leading off. The whole place was darker than it should have been, lending a creepy edge to the place that had Maya drawing her gun. Nothing about all of this felt safe.

"You said north corner?" Maya asked Samit.

"That's right. The signal was moving a little, but now it seems to be fixed in one spot."

Maya moved in that direction, checking each of the rooms she passed for signs of life. This level was a little cleaner than the one below, as if someone were using the filth of the bottom floor to discourage people from looking any closer.

"FBI," Maya called out. She couldn't imagine that she'd managed to enter the building without being seen or heard, and she would rather not run into someone trying to fight off what he saw as an intruder. "Is anyone there?"

There was no answer, but Maya didn't let that deter her. She kept moving forward to the room Samit had indicated. She pushed the door open and found herself in a bedroom. Half of one wall was piled high with old boxes. There was no sign of anyone there.

"You're sure this is the right spot?" Maya asked Samit.

"The phone should be right in front of you. About three or four yards."

The boxes. Maya stared at them, moving around slowly. Now she saw a hint of movement there, heard the scrape of a foot on the floorboards.

"Come out!" Maya demanded, keeping her gun leveled at the boxes.

A man slowly shuffled out from behind them with his hands raised. He was probably in his late thirties, with unkempt dark hair. He was wearing an army surplus jacket, jeans, and a t-shirt that might once have been white but now was anything but that.

"I haven't done anything," he said. "What do you want with me?"

"You made a call to report a dead body," Maya said. "A woman who had been strangled, murdered."

She saw his eyes widen.

"I never…"

"It was your phone. We traced it."

"I didn't touch her. It wasn't me. I just *found* her."

Maya could hear the fear in his voice. He obviously thought that she was planning to arrest him for murder.

"What's your name?" Maya demanded.

"Hank. I'm Hank Ward."

Maya's call with Samit was still open. She could hear the tech typing in the background.

"Hank Ward," Samit said. "A minor grifter. Arrests for petty theft, a few small cons. No violence."

Which fit with what Maya was currently thinking about the way things had happened.

"What did you take?" Maya asked Hank.

"What?" He wasn't very convincing.

"What did you take from the body?" Maya demanded. "I'll make it simple. You give me answers, or I'll arrest you."

"I…" Hank seemed to be calculating what he could get away with.

"I'll know if you lie."

He seemed to slump in on himself a little. "All right, all right. Here, take it. It's caused nothing but trouble for me anyway."

His hand went into his pocket, coming out with a round, shining shape: another moonstone.

"I couldn't even sell it, because I realized that it would make me look as if I killed her. I thought if I held onto it, eventually I could get something for it. But no, instead, *you're* here."

Maya reached out and snatched the stone from him.

"So you're not going to arrest me, right?" Hank said.

Maya shook her head. She didn't care about some low level grifter. She cared about catching a killer, and perhaps she'd just gotten the means to catch him. At the very least, she'd gotten the confirmation that this murder was a part of the pattern.

Now she just needed to work out where it fit, and what it all meant.

Taking the moonstone with her, Maya returned to her car. There, she used her laptop to pull up maps, starting to plot out the murders again. She put in Bella Simonetti's death, adding it along with the others. The straight line of kills that had been there before appeared again. This time though, it was more complete, with the murders appearing at neatly spaced intervals.

Now, Maya needed to know what that meant. There was a line, and there was also a direction of travel with it. There were clear intervals, what appeared to be very *precise* intervals.

Maya thought back to something Marco had said when looking at the crime scene around Laney Jackson's murder: that the killer seemed to have deliberately chosen to kill her there rather than closer to the bar. He'd been exact about where he killed his victims. The location was a part of his ritual, as if whatever he was trying to achieve wouldn't work unless he did everything precisely.

Maya had five locations now. Five stages along a journey. That left only the sixth step of the guru's process: the new moon, the dark moon, where everything went quiet.

Did that mean that there was going to be one more kill? One more woman from the retreat who was going to be murdered? If so, then Maya potentially had the information she needed to work out where that murder was going to take place.

If the murders were taking place at regularly spaced spots along a line, then as long as Maya was exact about her measurements, she should be able to extrapolate the next point along that line.

Maya zoomed in on her map, trying to get the scale to something she could work with. She tried to measure from spot to spot, realizing that if she was careful about the amount she zoomed, she could put one point on the very edge while the next was in the exact center of the screen. Maya drew a line along the map first, then worked her way along that line until the final murder was on the very edge of the screen. In theory, that should put the site of the next murder at the exact center of her screen.

Maya stared at it, trying to see what was there. The spot seemed to be outside the main city, on the far side of one of its lakes. Maya zoomed in further, trying to get a sense of what was there. There was a danger in trying to measure like this, that it wasn't precise, and it would be easy to get the wrong spot. In the middle of the city, being off even by a little would mean being several buildings out, but outside the city, in what appeared to be open space?

Maya needed to see this for herself, so she put directions to that spot into her car's GPS and set off. She wondered if she should call Marco. No, not yet. She still didn't have anything solid. More than that, she could imagine what he would say. He would be worried by her charging off after a pattern like this. He would suspect that Maya was clutching at straws, even if he didn't actually say it. Maya appreciated him as a partner, and she couldn't deny everything that she felt when it came to him, but she needed to be able to do this without being talked out of it.

Once she had something solid *then* she would call him.

Maya kept driving until she reached the lake and then took a road around it, keeping it on her left. The coordinates for the spot that she'd picked out on the map were getting closer by the second. There was a small side road and Maya took it since it seemed to take her in the right direction.

A few hundred yards further on, Maya found herself pulling up outside a house that had obviously been on this spot for a long time, right by the shore to the lake, looking out over it like a lone sentinel. It was timber built and slightly decaying, with missing tiles on the roof and walls overgrown on one side with ivy. The whole place looked completely uninviting, but right then Maya was incredibly grateful to see it. A landmark like this, in the spot that seemed to be the focal point of the entire ritual the killer was conducting?

This had to be the right spot, which meant that the pattern she'd found had given her the potential to find all the answers she needed. First, though, Maya needed to establish what this place was. She needed to see if there was anybody home and if there was, she needed to warn them about what might be about to happen. For all she knew, the killer could already be on his way to kill whatever young woman lived there.

Getting out of the car, Maya approached the house.

CHAPTER TWENTY SIX

Maya began by going up to the front door and hammering on it to get the attention of anyone inside.

"Hello? Is there anyone home? My name is Maya Gray. I'm with the FBI."

There was no answer from inside and now Maya found herself starting to worry. Was it possible that the killer had already been here? Was someone dying or dead in there? Was she too late?

Maya started to move around the outside of the house, checking the windows, looking for any sign of someone inside. She could see a perfectly pleasant family home in there, albeit one that looked a little dated. There was no sign of anyone that Maya could see.

They could still be there, though. Someone who had been killed might be out of sight upstairs. Even if there wasn't, then this was still the key location for this entire case. Maya kept moving around the house. There was a door at the back that wasn't secured. It would provide her with a way into the rest of the house.

She knew that it would be better to stand back and wait for a warrant, but everything about the pattern she'd found suggested that someone here might be in danger. Maya couldn't just wait while that risk existed. She had to do something, had to make sure that the occupants of the house were safe. If that got her into trouble later, then she would deal with it.

Her decision made, Maya opened the door and went inside, finding herself in a kitchen.

She wasn't sure what to make of the house within. Everything about it seemed dated, as if the contents had sat there for thirty or more years. Yet they weren't untouched. There were no layers of dust or cobwebs to contend with, just a strange kind of stillness and a décor that could have been the same for decades.

That was more than creepy enough, that sense that someone had just kept it like this, trapped in some version of the past, for all that time. They'd chosen to leave the house like this because everything about them was stuck in it.

"Is there anybody here?" Maya called out. "Do you need assistance?"

There was still no answer, which left her moving carefully and quietly through the house. There were a few pictures around the walls of a happy looking family, two parents and a young boy. There were more pictures of the boy growing up, then a couple of him as a man with different friends. A family home that had become the son's home, then?

That didn't fit with what Maya assumed was happening here. This killer had targeted young women so far, but this appeared to be a man's home. Maya needed to know more about what was going on. She continued to pad through the house, trying to make some kind of sense of the place.

She found cabinets in a dining room given over to New Age artifacts similar to those she had seen on her visit to the store. There were bookcases there too, filled with a mixture of books on self-help, spirituality, psychology, and alternative therapies.

Maya went through to what should have been a study and found that it was the only modern looking part of the house; it had been converted to what appeared to be a yoga and meditation room.

There were pictures up on the walls that made Maya stop and stare, because they had obviously been taken at the Lakeview Retreat. There was one of the man from the other pictures around the house standing next to Guru Alexander, shaking his hand. There were another couple of group photographs, all featuring the same man. The group's phases of the moon symbol sat in a frame next to the rest.

Maya tried to tell herself that it didn't mean anything, not when all the other victims had also had a connection to the retreat, but it was hard to stay objective about any of it. This was the end point of the sequence. This place mattered more than the rest of it.

Maya kept moving through the house. She checked the bedrooms, still wanting to make sure that there wasn't anyone hurt or dead there. Regardless of what she'd seen, that was still a risk, and one that Maya couldn't afford to overlook. Maya had to check each room carefully.

There was no sign of anyone, though. There was just the same strange stillness that pervaded the rest of the house. Maya returned downstairs and was going to call Samit to try to get more details on who owned the place when she saw the cellar door.

It was locked, but a key to it hung on a hook near the door. Maya took that down, opened the door and went down the basement steps carefully. They creaked with every step she took. When she found a light switch, Maya flicked it on, filling the space around her with the harsh light of a single bulb, shadows flickering across the walls.

Maya felt a mounting sense of worry about what she would find down there. What she saw made her stop in her tracks, trying to make sense of it.

Down there, Maya saw more of the materials from the retreat, only this was more like a shrine. Symbols for the stages of transformation stood over it, while next to it sat a large lump of what Maya could only assume was raw moonstone easily bigger than her fist, with a rock tumbler there beside it.

Maya got out her phone at once, calling Marco. He picked up quickly.

"Maya, where are you? I'm still not getting anywhere with the guru."

"Forget him," Maya said. "I need you to get to my location as quickly as you can. Bring police search teams with you."

"Why?" Marco asked. "What is it? What have you found?"

Maya paused for a second, wanting to be certain about it before she said the next part. She *was* certain, though, because there could be no other explanation.

"I think I'm standing in the killer's house."

*

Maya waited outside with Marco while the CSI teams started to tear the house apart. It was getting late now, the sun already dipping on the horizon. They'd been at it for hours, but for this part, Maya was prepared to be patient. There were probably half a dozen police cars around the place now, while search teams were combing the area around it, looking for anything that might be helpful.

Maya was holding onto the large lump of moonstone, keeping it as evidence. She wasn't about to let it out of her sight until she could get it examined and establish definitively that the moonstones found at the crime scenes had come from it.

"How did you even find this place?" Detective Keymer said.

Maya did her best to explain. "There's a pattern to the murders, a line, a progression. I think it's all part of the killer's ritual. Like he's building up power with every step."

She heard the detective make a small sound of disbelief.

"It doesn't matter that we all think it's not true," Maya said. "What matters is that the killer thinks it is. That he's prepared to kill for it."

"What do you think the point of this ritual is?" Marco asked.

“Judging by the books on display, and by his interest in the retreat, I’d say he’s trying to change something major about himself,” Maya said. She gestured to the house. “Everything in there is like it’s straight out of the past. He’s stuck in the past somehow, and he hates it.”

“Does it matter why he’s doing it?” Detective Keymer asked.

“Understanding some of it was what brought me here,” Maya pointed out. Beyond that, though, she was inclined to agree with the detective. What mattered was catching this killer, rather than understanding him. “It also matters that this place is the focal point of his ritual. Everything about it is focused here. This place is special to him.”

“Do we know who he is yet?” Marco asked. “Do we know who owns the house and who the guy in all the photographs is?”

Detective Keymer nodded. “The name we’re getting is Vincent Neward. He seems to have inherited this place from his grandparents. Parents died when he was a kid. He’s thirty-eight and has lived in Lagoon City all his life. No adult priors, but as a juvenile he got into trouble for attacking one of his classmates and for some animal cruelty.”

That sounded to Maya like a standard build up to greater violence. It suggested that Vincent had been on this path for longer than anyone had known.

“We brought someone else who might be able to provide some insight,” Detective Keymer said. He gestured to one of the patrol cars there. Maya made out the form of Guru Alexander sitting there in the back.

Maya wasn’t sure how cooperative the retreat’s leader was going to be, but if he could tell her anything that might get her closer to actually catching Vincent, then she had to try.

Maya headed over there with Marco beside her. She let the guru out of the car and he stood staring at the house.

“Guru Alexander, thank you for coming here,” she said.

“I wasn’t exactly given a choice,” he pointed out. “But now that I’m here, perhaps you could explain what’s going on? The police haven’t exactly been forthcoming.”

“We believe this is the house belonging to the real killer,” Maya said. “A man named Vincent Neward. Do you know him? He’s been to your retreat.”

“Vincent?” Guru Alexander said. He sounded briefly surprised, but the surprise quickly faded from his expression. “A troubled soul. He has been one of my students for a couple of years now. He spoke about parts of himself that he hated and wished to change. He said he was angry, that he would lash out at people. He wanted to stop that."

"He's done a lot more than lash out," Maya said. "He's planned and executed the murders of five women, all students of yours. My guess is that he met them at your retreat. *Would* he have met Heather Sullivan, Reba Andrews, Laney Jackson, Dianne Smith, and Bella Simonetti? Was he in the same groups at the same time as them?"

"The couple that I can remember, certainly," Guru Alexander said.

"Did he pay them special attention?"

"I… don't think so," the guru said. "He's always been friendly to some of the younger female guests, but he understood that there were boundaries within the retreat."

Within the retreat, but not outside. Even so it made sense that he might not have singled them out like that.

"Would he have known their addresses?" Maya asked.

"He might," Guru Alexander admitted. "He was so committed to our program and so eager to help out that he was permitted to help with some of our administrative aspects, helping to redesign some of our membership databases."

Meaning he would have everything he needed to find victims in the right areas to complete his ritual.

"Thank you," Maya said. "You've been very helpful. We'll have the local police make sure that you get back to your retreat safely."

Maya walked off in the direction of Marco's car. It was Vincent. There was no doubt about it now. Maya found herself wondering in that moment if just by establishing that she knew who the killer was that she'd done enough to win the Moonlight Killer's game. She'd found out the name of the killer. She'd cleared the Moonlight Killer of the crime and found out who the real culprit was.

Somehow, she doubted that was enough for him. He would want her to catch Vincent, and that might still prove anything but easy.

"Keymer will put out an APB," Marco said, obviously guessing what Maya was thinking. "While there will be plenty of cops here."

"He won't come back here," Maya said. "Not with so many people around."

"So what do you plan to do to catch him?" Marco asked.

"I'm not sure yet," Maya said. "But I want to hang onto the moonstone. I think it's the only thing in all this that means anything to him. I want to keep it close until I can get it logged into an evidence room back at the local PD."

Marco nodded. “We’ll head back there. The local cops can finish up here. They’ll catch him, Maya.”

Maya hoped so. This wasn’t done yet. Not until Vincent Neward was in her custody. Until that moment, the Moonlight Killer’s clock was still ticking.

CHAPTER TWENTY SEVEN

Vincent crouched in bushes well away from his house, feeling fear and anger competing within him for dominance. He tried to use a pranayama breathing technique from yoga to still his mind, but there was only so much that it could do right then.

The police were at his home. They were searching it. That meant that they knew what he'd done.

They wouldn't understand. They wouldn't see the necessity of everything that he'd done. They wouldn't see that it was the only way to stop all of this. To truly change who he was.

Vincent crouched lower, watching the search teams move across his property like ants. He assumed that it wouldn't be long before they found the bodies of his grandparents buried in the yard. Not his first kills, but certainly his first human ones. They'd called him a monster for some of the things he'd done. They'd tried to beat it out of him, and he'd… snapped.

His parents had died more naturally if a car accident could be called natural. Vincent sometimes found himself wondering if he would have been different if they hadn't died. More than one of his therapists had tried to explore that question with him, trying to suggest to Vincent that it was what he did with is life now that mattered. Vincent always found that annoying. He *wanted* to be different; they just never gave him the tools to change.

Vincent wasn't proud of any of the things he'd done. He hated himself for who he was. It was what made transforming into someone new so important.

Vincent could see the cops fanning out around the house. A part of him wanted to find a way in there, trying to get to the precious moonstone within, but he couldn't see a way past all of them. Soon, they would be close enough that he would have to abandon his hiding place and leave.

The thought of doing so without the moonstone was almost physically painful for him. It was the key to his transformation.

He'd tried other options. He'd tried to change himself in every possible way over the years. He'd tried therapy, drugs both medical and otherwise, the distractions of alcohol and women, a dozen different psychologists espousing everything from Jungian dream analysis to cognitive behavioral therapy and hypnosis. He'd even subjected himself to electroshock therapy.

None of it had worked. None of it had changed who he was. None of it made the violent impulses disappear, and when he held them back, the stress of it felt as though it was going to make his head explode.

Vincent had only found answers when he'd gone to work on his problems with Guru Alexander at his retreat. The work there had done a little to sooth him, but the real power was in the transformative process. The stages of the moon.

Vincent could see Guru Alexander there now, talking to a tall man and a woman in a dark suit. Vincent thought he'd seen her on the news, an FBI agent there to re-investigate one of his kills. If the guru was talking to them, then either he was betraying Vincent or he needed to be saved from them. Either way, the temptation was to go over to them to try to break him free of them.

Vincent got control over himself with an effort. He'd worked so hard on control. Almost as hard as he'd worked on the design of the ritual. Six phases of the moon. Six facets of himself placed into a moonstone, transferred into another, and then destroyed as they died. A cumulative wash of power that, with the completion of the sixth death, would flow into him and cleanse him.

He'd chosen his victims carefully from among those in the guru's group, picking out those he could get to the correct places at the correct times. That they'd all been young women… well, in that one thing he'd given in to the facet of himself that he was trying to change. Besides, it meant that they had so much potential. He transferred his old self into them through the moonstones, and their potential for a fresh start would flow into him when the ritual was complete.

He had to complete it. He'd been out trying to find someone suitable when the police had come. For this last kill, he'd reasoned, he could simply trick someone back to his home, or even kidnap her if needed, but he'd wanted it to be perfect. That perfectionism had saved him from being caught.

It was fate, but he couldn't leave it at that. He had to keep going. He had to finish this.

It occurred to him for the briefest of moments that he could just run. He could abandon everything here and disappear. The police would be looking for him so, logically, it would be better to get far away.

But he couldn't. He couldn't just leave now. He had to find a way to get to his moonstone. He'd picked up the raw moonstone on a trip into the mountains, hiking for days and trying to clear his mind. He needed it, needed to tumble the stone he used for the ritual in order to put more of himself into it.

Then he saw it. Even at this distance, Vincent wasn't going to miss it. It was unmistakable. The FBI agent had his moonstone in her hand. She was taking it from him, taking his power. Vincent saw her getting into a car with the tall man she'd been speaking with.

Vincent hurried back to his own waiting vehicle, starting to follow them. The house didn't matter, not now. He needed his moonstone back. He needed to finish this, his way.

CHAPTER TWENTY EIGHT

"Is there any sign of him yet?" Maya demanded.

Maya sat in the Lagoon City PD, trying to coordinate the hunt for Vincent Neward. She had a map of the city set out in front of her, a board to one side containing every detail that they'd found out about him so far. There were pictures of him up there along with notes of key locations in his life: the places he'd been on vacation, the location data they'd been able to pull from his social media.

"Not yet," Marco replied.

Marco and Detective Keymer were in there with them, each making a separate phone call. They'd been working on this for hours now, trying to make sure that there was no chance of Vincent getting away.

"Where are we with the search?" Maya asked. She needed to know that they were making progress on this. They only had one more day to catch him, but a manhunt could take weeks. They had to find a way to catch up before then, or lives were at risk.

"I have an APB out three states wide," Detective Keymer said. "We're watching major highways in case he tries to leave."

"What else?" Maya asked.

"I'm just calling Samit," Marco said. "He's trying to track Vincent's phone, but it looks like he ditched it. Samit's sending through a request to the NSA for voice recognition, so if he acquires another one we'll know about it, but that will take time."

It was a sensible, solid move, but right then Maya suspected that they needed more. "Are we talking to any family or friends in case he runs there?"

"As far as we can tell, he doesn't have any family left," Detective Keymer said. "And he never had many close friends. We'll send cars around to all the ones he *does* have, and we're watching the retreat in case he goes there."

Maya nodded. That was a good thought. The ritual he was conducting would still be important to him. That also meant that there was a good chance that he might try to return to his home to complete the ritual there. They needed to be ready to deal with that possibility, but it also presented them with an opportunity.

"I want you to scale back the police presence at his home," Maya said. "Or at least appear to. There's a chance that he's just waiting for an opportunity to try to slip in there."

"I'll tell my guys to keep a lower profile," Detective Keymer said. "I've also put in calls to local reporters. Vincent's face is going to be all over the local news within the hour."

It felt like they had every base covered, leaving Vincent with nowhere to run. Even so, Maya found herself staring at the map again, trying to think of what else she could do to try to bring Vincent to justice sooner.

"I think you have everything covered," Marco said. "We'll get him, Maya. A guy like this, he's not used to being on the run. He'll slip up, and slip up quickly. All we have to do is wait."

"Yes, but how long?" Maya asked. That was the problem, when they only had a day left.

"We'll get him," Marco said again. "For now, though, there's nothing useful we can do here, and it's getting late. I think we should head back to the hotel and let the local PD search for him tonight. If he's not caught by morning, then we'll be fresh to try to think of something else."

"I don't like the idea of just going back to the hotel and sleeping," Maya said. "I could take a break for an hour, then go out on patrol."

Detective Keymer stepped in then. "Your partner's right, Agent Gray. Sitting here staring at that map isn't helping. Let us handle this tonight. I'll stay awake to run it. Tomorrow, you can take over again. That way, we know there's someone fresh on it. We *will* catch him."

Maya could see that she was outvoted on this one. They weren't going to let her run this through the night even though this was her case.

"Ok," she said. "But we're starting again *early* tomorrow."

*

They headed back to the hotel. Maya hated having to give up like this for the night, but she knew that Marco and Detective Keymer were right. She tried to remind herself that they had all day tomorrow in which to catch the killer.

She and Marco paused in the corridor outside their rooms. Marco put a hand on her shoulder and Maya could feel the strength there, the reassurance in the touch.

"You've done it, Maya," he said. "You've found the guy who did this. Everything else is just a matter of time."

Maya forced a smile. "You make me sound like I'm some kind of genius."

"I don't know about genius, but you *are* amazing."

He leaned in towards her and in that moment Maya found herself doing the same. They kissed, deeply and slowly. Maya could feel herself pressed tight against him, feeling every ridge of muscle there beneath his shirt. It would have been so easy right then to invite him to spend the night with her in her room, but Maya knew that she couldn't, not now, not here.

She finished the kiss instead, reluctantly pulling back from him.

"We still need to be up early," she said. "And I suspect that if we keep going, neither one of us is going to be particularly well rested come morning."

That got a smile from Marco, but it was a wan one. He'd obviously been hoping that this would go further. Maya could definitely understand the feeling. Only her need to make sure that the case was under control stopped her from inviting him in even now.

"I guess you have a point," Marco said. "I'll see you in the morning, Maya. Maybe we'll revisit this when we get back to D.C."

"I'd like that," Maya assured him. She suspected that it was a possibility that would be in her dreams. At least, she hoped it would be. It would be a definite improvement over most of her dreams these days.

Maya watched Marco go into his room, then went into her own. She took off her jacket and stowed her gun by the bed for the night.

It was only then that she saw the elegant square of cardboard sitting on top of her bag, waiting there for her like a slap to the face.

Maya stared at it in disbelief and anger that the Moonlight Killer would get the postcard there, as if to prove that he could get to her anywhere. She hated him even more for that, even as Maya knew what that meant: the Moonlight Killer was sending her another message.

She snatched up the postcard, determined to make sense of it all and looking it over. There was no writing on this one, just a picture of a bunny rabbit, sitting in the bottom of a large hourglass.

With that image, Maya felt a wave of tension building up inside her, any attempt to relax fleeing from her all at once. The message was obvious: the clock was still running, the investigation didn't finish until Vincent Neward was in custody. Maya had suspected that anyway, but to have it confirmed meant that the pressure was on now.

She had one more day, that was all, in which to catch up to the man she knew to be the killer.

Maya thought about calling out to Marco to let him know about the postcard, but no, it didn't change anything and whoever had delivered it would be long gone by now. It would be better to let him get some sleep.

Maya could definitely do with some rest too, but as she lay back on the hotel bed, she quickly realized that wasn't going to happen. At least not yet. She was too wired to sleep, with her brain still running through every aspect of the case. It seemed to her that there was an answer to where Vincent would be out there somewhere, if only she could find a way to work it out. Her brain went into overdrive, trying to calculate how a killer like Vincent would respond to this situation, but the truth was that she didn't know.

Maya sighed and stood up, grabbing her jacket. She wasn't going to sleep while her brain was still trying to work everything out. The best thing to do was probably to take a walk try to think and let all the ideas work their way out of her system. Maya knew that if she just lay there staring at the ceiling nothing was going to get better.

She headed downstairs and then out into the night air. The stars were out now, and Maya found herself looking around for the moon as she walked, out along the street and then down towards the shore of the nearest lake. It was dark tonight though, the new moon making it look absent.

Thoughts of the moon made her think of the Moonlight Killer. He was still out there somewhere, maybe even stalking another victim, getting ready for the next full moon. Even now, Maya didn't know as much as she would like about him.

What *did* she know? Not much. That he was clever, that he was dangerous. That he didn't hesitate to kill and that he was probably unstable. She was pretty sure that he was former special forces, whereas she'd been military intelligence. Other than that, she didn't even have a general physical description for him beyond the "average height, in shape" that had been all the kidnapped women could tell past the masks and nondescript clothes he wore.

Maya forced her thoughts away from the Moonlight Killer and back to Vincent Neward. His methods might be very similar to those of the Moonlight Killer, but he was ultimately very different. Maya couldn't imagine the Moonlight Killer wanting to change himself, certainly couldn't imagine him using some kind of ritual to do it. He was organized and precise, while Maya couldn't imagine him leaving a calling card like the moonstone behind. Even his moments of whimsy in the postcards seemed more calculated than anything Vincent might do.

Vincent… well, he was a man adrift right now. He'd been denied the chance to finish his ritual. His face was all over the news and his car was impounded. He would be on foot. Maya half expected a call at any minute to say he'd been picked up by a highway patrol, trying to walk all the way to Baltimore or D.C.

Except that another part of her didn't think that fit with what he wanted from all of this. This was a man who had been determined enough to plan six murders, spacing them out so that he would be able to get them at the times and places he wanted. That wasn't a man who would give up easily.

He would make some kind of attempt to get his lump of moonstone, or to find a replacement. They would have to keep the main stone carefully guarded, and circulate his description to any jewelers in the area.

Would he make a try at the precinct? Maybe, but a worse possibility occurred to Maya. She'd been the one to find the moonstone in his house. She'd been the one to take it from there. If Vincent found that out somehow…

Maya started back towards the hotel, hurrying now, feeling uneasy and defenseless. Her gun was back in her room because she hadn't thought she'd need it for an evening stroll.

A sound came from the dark: a man's footsteps. There was a figure there in the street, between Maya and the hotel, lurking at the mouth of an alley. As Maya saw him, he stepped forward, into the glow of a streetlight. It allowed Maya to make out his features.

"You know who I am?" Vincent asked.

"I know. You're under arrest, Vincent."

He shook his head. "I don't think so. I think you're out here alone. I think you don't have any backup."

"I can still take you down," Maya said.

"We'll see," he replied. He was holding a length of what looked like old pipe in his right hand. Presumably he'd found it somewhere while he was looking for her. "You interfered. You took what was mine. I *saw* you take my moonstone. I need it. I have to finish the ritual. So I think… I think I'll take my moonstone back and finish it with you."

Maya braced herself, and Vincent charged forward at her.

CHAPTER TWENTY NINE

Maya wished more than anything that she'd brought her gun with her for her walk. If she'd had it with her, she could have drawn it and ended this in less than a second, taking down the man who had killed so many women.

As it was, she had to brace herself for his rush, trying to work out what to do against the length of pipe he was swinging towards her head. It wasn't the kind of weapon she could block because that would mean a broken arm. Instead, she had to try to avoid the most dangerous part of the swing.

She guessed that Vincent would expect her to step back, trying to avoid the blow, hoping that the momentum of his charge would barrel her over, letting him land blow after blow before she could recover.

Maya stepped in instead, ducking inside the blow, taking some of it on her left shoulder and ignoring the pain while she jabbed a palm up into his jaw, hitting him with her full weight behind it. Her fingers jabbed at his eyes, but he managed to jerk his head back.

Vincent leapt back away from Maya. She tried to chase him, trying to stay in close, but he lashed out at her with the pipe he held so violently that Maya had to give him space. Maya darted past two parked cars, trying to put some cover between her and Vincent.

The only problem with that was that she had to engage him at some point. If this had been some random attacker, Maya might have been able to run, escaping or getting back to a weapon. It wasn't random, though. This was the man she'd been hunting for days now, the man she had to bring to justice so a woman's life wouldn't end.

Maya couldn't run. If she ran, she might never find him again. He was there in front of her and she *had* to find a way to bring him down.

"My moonstone," Vincent said. "Where is my moonstone? I know you have it."

"I don't," Maya replied. The moonstone was safely hidden away in the LCPD's evidence lock up by now.

Vincent brought the pipe around to smash the windshield of one of the cars between them. Its alarm blared into the night air, but Maya didn't hold out much hope of it attracting anyone who might help her.

People's main response to alarms was to ignore them, and if they called the police, it was because it had irritated them by running for too long.

By the time they got around to doing that, she might be long dead.

"Don't lie to me!" he snarled. "Where is my moonstone? Without it, the voices… they're too much…"

"Why don't you put the weapon down, Vincent, and we can talk about it?"

Vincent just followed her around the car. Maya kept it between the two of them, using it as a barrier to stop him from reaching her with the pipe.

"You think I'm going to fall for that?" Vincent demanded. "I'm going to kill you. I'm going to take back my moonstone, finish the ritual using *you* and everything will be all right."

"Except that I don't have the moonstone, Vincent," Maya insisted. She was following his movements now, trying to judge the best moment in which to act.

"You're lying!" He smashed another window.

That was when Maya saw her chance. She leapt onto the hood of the car, ran over the roof, and flung herself at Vincent, crashing into him.

He swung the pipe, but this close, there wasn't enough space to generate momentum. The blows were easy to shrug off, with Maya's weight bearing him to the ground. Down there, they could fight without Vincent having the room to bring his weapon to bear.

Maya was on top of him. She hit him once, then wrenched at his arm, trying to get the length of metal pipe out of his grip. Maya put both hands into it, managing to wrench the pipe clear, sending it spinning away to land in the street.

The movement cost her, though. By committing so much to one side, Maya had created a situation where she couldn't stop Vincent from going the other way. Suddenly, he was moving behind her.

Maya tried to turn to face him, but she couldn't move fast enough on the ground to keep up with him. He was scrambling behind her with all the speed of someone who had done it to many victims before. Maya realized in that moment what was going to happen next. She'd been focused on the metal pipe, but that wasn't the weapon that he'd used to murder five women.

Maya saw the rope coming into her field of vision and threw up a hand to try to block it. She managed to get a couple of fingers in the way, but the strength pulling the rope back towards her neck was greater than anything she could have imagined.

“You’ve ruined it,” Vincent snarled as he hauled on the rope. “You’ve ruined the ritual. But I can salvage it. I can kill you. I can change everything.”

Maya didn’t have the breath to answer. She threw elbows back with her left arm, while her right hand was agony as it tried to keep the rope away from her throat. Maya kept striking back at Vincent, trying to hit him hard enough to create some space that she could use to escape.

It didn’t work. Maya could feel the rope slipping past her fingers and she tried to scrabble to hold on, but it was past an instant later and the rope was cutting into her neck.

Maya couldn’t breathe, couldn’t think. She felt herself starting to panic, her hands going to the rope even though she knew she needed to deal with the man holding it rather than with the rope itself. She kicked out at him, then tried to throw herself sharply to one side, hoping that the combination would be enough to break Vincent’s grip on her.

If anything, it only made the rope tighter.

“Do you have much potential, Agent?” Vincent demanded as he pulled on the rope. “Will your death add much to the others? It doesn’t matter; the power from the others is what counts. You’re just the key unlocking the door to it.”

He was pressed so tightly to her that there wasn’t even an inch between them. He was as close as a lover would have been, but there was nothing tender about the way he dragged the rope into Maya’s neck. He was strangling her expertly, efficiently, not giving Maya any chance to fight back successfully.

Maya could feel the pressure in her head building as the blood fought to get to her brain. She gasped for air but there was none to be had.

She found herself thinking about her sister, trapped at the hands of the Moonlight Killer. If Maya died, would he let her go, or would he count that as Maya failing? Would he kill all the women he still held as his captives? Maya didn’t have to think to know the answer to that. He was a serial killer, ruthless in his application of the rules of his “game.” If Maya died, then so would all his captives, including her sister.

That gave Maya the impetus she needed to fight on, yet it still didn’t do any good. She didn’t have the strength left to fight. She could see the world starting to fade around the edges as her consciousness closed in on itself. As much as Maya tried to fight to survive, she was dying.

She found herself thinking of Marco in that moment. She found herself thinking of their kisses and the time they’d spent together. She found herself imagining what it would be like to have him there with her in her last moments, she even imagined him standing over her there, looking down at her and…

…wait, she wasn't imagining that part, was she? Marco was there, looking both furious and protective. He'd obviously followed her outside, wanting to talk, or just as unable to sleep as Maya was.

He slammed into Vincent, ripping him away from Maya. With his grip on the strangling rope gone, Maya was able to breathe again. She sucked in great gasps of air, feeling her consciousness coming back to her.

While she did it, Marco and Vincent were off to her side, exchanging blows. The killer swung hard, catching Marco in the side with a fist. Marco retaliated with a one-two, followed by a kick that sent Vincent sprawling.

Maya saw Marco start to close the gap on him, but even as he did so, Maya spotted Vincent reaching for something in the road. Too late, she realized that it was the metal pipe.

"Marco, watch out!" she yelled, but Vincent was already swinging the pipe. She heard the moment when it connected with Marco's skull, sending him to the ground, obviously dazed.

Vincent got up and hit him again. Then again. Marco was still struggling to rise, but every time he did so, Vincent hit him.

"You want to interfere? You want to stop me completing my ritual? You deserve to die, just like her!"

The sight of Marco being struck like that seemed to light some kind of fire in Maya, one born of pure fury. She drove herself to her feet. The rope that Vincent had been using to strangle her was still around her neck. Maya took it in her hand and charged forward.

She whipped it out, wrapping it around Vincent's arm even as he drew the metal pipe back to strike at Marco again. She pulled with all her strength, stopping the blow from falling.

She kicked out at the back of one of his knees, buckling it. She wrenched the pipe from Vincent's hand again, sending it clattering to the road once more. Vincent tried to turn towards her, but Maya yanked on the rope, pulling him off balance. She used that moment of unbalance to hit him, striking him on the side of the jaw and knocking him further back.

Maya lashed out again, knocking Vincent down this time. Marco was there with her now, but even with him there, it was hard work trying to hold Vincent down. He thrashed about wildly, lashing out at both of them, seemingly at random so that Maya had to fight to keep her grip on him.

She didn't have any handcuffs on her, so she used the rope Vincent had used to try to strangle her, forcing his hands together and then tying them in place. That made him a little easier to hold onto him, but even so, she and Marco had to wait for several minutes before he finally went still.

"Vincent Neward," Maya said. "You're under arrest."

CHAPTER THIRTY

Back home, and Maya was frustrated, sitting in her office in the FBI's building, waiting for the release of the woman she knew she'd earned by capturing Vincent Neward.

"There should have been a postcard by now," Maya said to Marco for what had to be the sixth or seventh time. She knew it, but she still couldn't keep herself from saying it.

"There will be," Marco reassured her.

"I hope so."

Maya couldn't stand the fact that she had to play along with the Moonlight Killer's game just to get him to release the women he was holding captive. She couldn't stand the thought that all it would take was for the serial killer to change his mind about how he worked and her sister would be dead, all at one man's whim.

She couldn't stand the waiting, when the Moonlight Killer had given *her* so little time this time.

It was obvious, too, that she wasn't the only one frustrated.

"Where's the postcard?" Harris demanded, as he stepped into Maya's office. He was an avuncular man in his mid-fifties, with balding hair closely shaved, an expensive suit and normally a sense of being there for everyone who needed him. Just recently, though, Maya's boss had become a thorn in her side, wanting to run the whole kidnapping case his way, not hers. His way included charging after the kidnapper at every turn, in defiance of the Moonlight Killer's instructions not to do that.

"We're still waiting for it, sir," Maya replied. "The kidnapper has been inconsistent about his timing before."

"He's also killed his hostages before, even after you've succeeded at his little game," Harris pointed out. There was something almost hungry about his expression, like a shark sensing blood in the water. "If that happens again, Gray, then this taskforce is done. We put up with your approach because it's getting results, but the moment that isn't true, this is done."

Harris had made no secret of his desire to take the case back into the cold case department. He certainly made no secret of his dislike for Maya's approach to the case.

The worst part was that Maya couldn't exactly counter what he was saying. Two of the women the Moonlight Killer had kidnapped had died. He claimed that one had killed herself, while the other had been trying to escape, but Maya had only limited ways of verifying that. It fit with what his other hostages had said when they'd been released, but maybe he'd manipulated them. Maybe he was killing whenever he couldn't control himself enough to stop himself from doing it.

"For now, at least," Maya said. "I'm in charge of this task force, and that means-"

She didn't finish that, because in that moment Samit ran in. Maya could see from the expression on his face that it was serious, and she saw why only a moment later. There was a postcard in his hand, one that he threw down on Maya's desk with an expression that said he understood exactly how important it was. Everyone in the department did, by this point.

"It's here!"

Maya snatched the postcard up. On the reverse, the Moonlight Killer had written the briefest of messages.

Dear Maya,

Congratulations. Another one solved, and so quickly. I do so love the forest this time of year. Better get to her before any animals do.

The front of the postcard was hand drawn the way all his postcards seemed to be, this one featuring an image of a cartoon bunny rabbit tied to a tree.

"Is that it?" Marco said. "Just 'she's tied to a tree somewhere?' It's not enough to find anyone."

"Look under the picture," Maya pointed out. "Do you see those faint lines there? I think that's a section of map. Those are contour lines."

"But how are we meant to find where this is?" Harris asked. He was staring at the postcard now. "There are no placenames or obvious landmarks on it."

"It depends how accurate he's been," Maya said. "And my guess is that for this, he's been *very* accurate. Samit, can you take this map, copy it, and then search for this section on our systems? My guess is that it will match up exactly with a more standard map, and then we can use *that* to find out where this woman has been left."

Samit nodded. "I'll try. It will probably take a few minutes."

"Be as quick as you can," Maya said. "There's a woman out there somewhere in danger. In the meantime, we need to organize EMTs to go with us to pick her up."

"I'll get on that," Marco said.

It was hard, waiting while Samit fed the information from the map into his computer. Maya could see the system cycling through fragments of maps, processing millions of them at a speed that was almost impossible to follow. Maya willed it to find something, because there was a woman waiting out there, exposed to the elements, vulnerable to any animals that wandered past.

"I've got it!" Samit declared, the screen fixing on a single section of map. He zoomed out, showing that it was maybe thirty miles from D.C. "I have the location."

"We need to get there," Maya said. "Right now."

*

According to the map, the location of the missing woman was inside a section of woodland somewhere in Virginia. Maya was currently making her way through it, along with a whole tactical team of FBI agents and an EMT team. The trees closed in around her, so that it seemed that there was almost no light to be found.

Marco was at Maya's left, moving forward carefully, in case there were traps. The Moonlight Killer had shown before just how much he loved to leave traps behind and, even if Maya had successfully completed one of his cases, she wasn't about to take chances.

The hardest part was trying to find the location that the postcard indicated on the ground. The contour lines might have matched the map precisely, but that didn't mean that there were any landmarks that Maya could follow at ground level. All she could do was try to follow a GPS bearing on her phone, hoping that it led to the right spot.

They were closing in, the GPS signal seeming to lead them to a small clearing in the middle of the forest. Maya stepped into it confidently, fully expecting to see a woman tied there waiting for them. Instead, though, there was nothing.

"Where is she?" Marco asked.

"I don't know."

"Are you sure that this is the right spot?"

"I don't *know* Marco, all right? I thought this was the spot, but all I have to go on is the GPS."

She could feel her own anger and frustration building. The Moonlight Killer had sent her on another chase, obviously trying to see how well Maya deciphered his clues, and Maya was getting sick of it.

She didn't like being controlled by him, didn't like being made to do whatever he wanted just to ensure the safety of his captives.

She hated being his puppet, but she didn't have any choice. She had to save these women. She had to save her sister.

"Maya, I'm just trying to help," Marco said.

"If you want to help, check the map. Make sure that we're in the right spot." Maya didn't like snapping at Marco, but she needed answers about the right way to go. She needed to know that she hadn't been lied to by the Moonlight Killer.

"I think we're in the right place," Marco said, after a moment or two.

"Then where is she? Where's the woman he promised to release?"

Maya spotted the answer to that a second later, in a flicker of movement further in the trees.

Maya ran for it and a few seconds later found herself looking at a young woman. She was slightly built, red-haired, and pale. She was also both dirty and bruised from her time in the forest. Her hand was chained to the trunk of the nearest tree and she was wearing a dull gray jumpsuit, the same as the other women Maya had rescued. She looked exhausted and dehydrated, as if she'd been there for some time.

She looked up at Maya as she approached.

"Are you… are you Maya? Megan's sister?"

Maya nodded. "I am."

"He… he said you would come to find me. I didn't believe it. I thought… I was sure I was going to die."

"When did he leave you out here?" Maya asked.

"A day ago? More?"

So he'd done it even before Maya had closed the case? She realized that was probably the Moonlight Killer's way of ensuring that this woman would die if Maya failed. All he had to do was keep from telling Maya where she was and she would die of exposure, or hunger, or thirst. It was a horrific way to die.

"What's your name?" Maya asked her.

"Saoirse."

"We'll have you out of here soon, Saoirse," Maya promised her. She gestured for Marco to come forward and start working on the chain that held her to the tree. From behind her, she could see the EMTs coming forward, obviously ready to check the other woman over.

That didn't leave Maya with much time. "Saoirse, can you tell me anything, anything at all, about the man who has been keeping you captive?"

"I… no, he wore a mask."

"Please, try to think," Maya insisted. "What about the place you were being held? Can you remember anything about where it was? Do you remember anything about the journey here from there?"

"No… I'm sorry."

"Please, try to think," Maya said. "Any detail you can remember might allow us to find the others."

"I can't remember anything," Saoirse said. Her eyes were red with the beginnings of tears.

"Maya," Marco said in a warning tone.

"Think carefully," Maya said. "Any detail you can remember might be the one that lets me fid the others and that brings the man who did this to justice."

"I can't *remember* anything," Saoirse said.

"If you just-"

"*Maya,*" Marco said. "She's been through a lot and she obviously doesn't remember anything. Give her a chance to rest."

Maya wanted to argue, but the EMTs were there then. They managed to get Saoirse free of the chain that held her, moving her onto a gurney to start to move her back through the forest towards safety.

Maya wanted to go to her even then to try to get any information she could. The others had all provided fragments, either passed on by Megan or things that they'd picked up by accident.

Marco was there in front of her then. "Maya, that's enough. You're obsessing over this."

"I'm not obsessing, I'm doing my job," Maya said.

"It's your job to harass a woman who has only just escaped captivity?"

"It's my job to catch a killer before he kills anyone else," Maya said. "Before he kills my *sister*."

"And you will," Marco said. "But not like this."

"That's not your decision to make, Marco," Maya snapped back. She couldn't help herself. "Whatever we might be to each other outside of work, *in* work, I'm your boss. I'm the one in charge of the taskforce."

"You're going to play *that* card?" Marco demanded.

Maya knew she'd gone too far, but she couldn't stop herself. "If it means saving my sister, I'll play any card I have to. If you don't like it, go back to D.C."

"Maybe I will," Marco said and walked off.

Maya didn't watch him go. He'd be back. Right then, though, she had to focus on doing whatever she could to try to find the location of the spot where the Moonlight Killer was holding the women he'd kidnapped. That was where her sister was, which meant that was where she needed to go.

To find that, Maya would do whatever she had to do. She would make it up to Marco later.

CHAPTER THIRTY ONE

Marco was at home in his apartment, trying not to think about Maya. She was infuriating, impossible, but also brilliant. He'd never met anyone as amazing, as driven as she was, yet that drive seemed to spill over into obsession all too easily.

His D.C. apartment was as homey as he'd been able to make it in just a few weeks, with throws on the floor and pictures on the wall to try to add an element of comfort. Marco wasn't a guy who could get by with a minimalist place that he barely spent any time in.

Unlike Maya.

Somehow, every thought led back to her and had almost from the moment that he'd met her. That he had deep, tangled feelings for her was undeniable. Unfortunately, so was the complexity of their situation. What if they couldn't work together? What if it was too difficult for them to do that and still have any kind of involvement with one another?

Marco couldn't stand the thought of that. He wanted them to have everything, to be able to work together, to be partners, to be more than that. Yet today had shown how difficult that was and Marco knew that it wasn't going to get any easier. Not until all of this was solved.

Yet he was determined to stay by Maya's side. He would be there for her. He would help her to catch the Moonlight Killer and save her sister.

Marco was still thinking about that when a knock came on his apartment door.

"Marco, it's me."

Maya's voice. Marco rushed over to the door. Did she want to talk about what had happened earlier? Did she want more than that? Marco didn't know, but the sound of her voice was enough to make him throw open the door.

A figure came in, tossing aside a cheap voice recorder. He was athletically muscled and almost Marco's height, but that was all Marco could tell about him. He was wearing a dark hoodie with a mask underneath, while even his hands were covered by gloves. Marco realized that he'd been fooled.

One of those hands held something. Too late, Marco realized that it was a stun gun.

The weapon jabbed towards him and Marco tried to dodge away from it. He was too slow, the crackle of electricity sounding as the stun gun made contact with his side. Agony flooded through Marco. Worse, his muscles refused to obey him, the jolting power of the electricity sending his whole nervous system into spasm.

His attacker knocked him to the floor, then kicked him, hard enough that Marco was sure he felt ribs break. When Marco tried to crawl in the direction of his waiting gun, the attacker used the stun gun on him again, bringing him down. He followed it up with a couple of punches to Marco's skull that left him tasting blood and seeing stars.

He rolled onto his back, staring up at his attacker, trying to catch his breath. The assailant didn't give him a chance to recover, though, because he passed Marco's legs in a single swift movement, jumping on top of Marco and pinning him down. Another jolt from the stun gun sent a fresh wave of agony through Marco.

A couple of elbows followed it, sending him to the brink of unconsciousness.

"Don't pass out just yet," his attacker said. "We're just getting started."

He stood up then and put the stun gun away. He walked almost calmly over to the spot where Marco's service weapon sat. He lifted it, pointing it straight at Marco. Marco tried to move, tried to avoid it, but he couldn't do anything. He was helpless.

The shot was deafeningly loud in the confines of the apartment, and agony bloomed in Marco. He'd been hit, somewhere in the stomach.

The attacker tossed the gun away then and turned for the door, leaving Marco behind to bleed to death.

NOW AVAILABLE!

GIRL EIGHT: HUNTED
(A Maya Gray FBI Suspense Thriller—Book 8)

12 cold cases. 12 kidnapped women. One diabolical serial killer. In this riveting suspense thriller, a brilliant FBI agent faces a deadly challenge: decipher the mystery before each one is murdered.

"Molly Black has written a taut thriller that will keep you on the edge of your seat… I absolutely loved this book and can't wait to read the next book in the series!"
—Reader review for Girl One: Murder

In the Maya Gray series (which begins with Book #1—GIRL ONE: MURDER), FBI Special Agent Maya Gray, 39, has seen it all. She's one of BAU's rising stars and the go-to agent for hard-to-crack serial cases. When she receives a handwritten postcard promising to release 12 kidnapped women if she will solve 12 cold cases, she assumes it's a hoax.

Until the note mentions that, among the captives, is her missing sister.

Maya, shaken, is forced to take it seriously. The cases she's up against are some of the most difficult the FBI has ever seen. But the terms of his game are simple: If Maya solves a case, he will release one of the girls.

And if she fails, he will end a life.

In GIRL EIGHT: HUNTED (book #8), a new serial killer is leaving a mysterious signature at each crime scene: a mirror.

Maya struggles to crack the riddle and decipher its significance. Why a mirror?

Is the killer hinting at himself?

Or could it mean that he is targeting Maya next?

A complex psychological crime thriller full of twists and turns and packed with heart-pounding suspense, the MAYA GRAY mystery series will make you fall in love with a brilliant new female protagonist and keep you turning pages late into the night. It is a perfect addition for fans of Robert Dugoni, Rachel Caine, Melinda Leigh or Mary Burton.

Book #9 in the series—GIRL NINE: GONE—is now also available.

"I binge read this book. It hooked me in and didn't stop till the last few pages… I look forward to reading more!"
—Reader review for Found You

"I loved this book! Fast-paced plot, great characters and interesting insights into investigating cold cases. I can't wait to read the next book!"
—Reader review for Girl One: Murder

"Very good book… You will feel like you are right there looking for the kidnapper! I know I will be reading more in this series!"
—Reader review for Girl One: Murder

"This is a very well written book and holds your interest from page 1… Definitely looking forward to reading the next one in the series, and hopefully others as well!"
—Reader review for Girl One: Murder

"Wow, I cannot wait for the next in this series. Starts with a bang and just keeps going."
—Reader review for Girl One: Murder

“Well written book with a great plot, one that will keep you up at night. A page turner!”
—Reader review for Girl One: Murder

“A great suspense that keeps you reading… can't wait for the next in this series!”
—Reader review for Found You

“Sooo soo good! There are a few unforeseen twists… I binge read this like I binge watch Netflix. It just sucks you in.”
—Reader review for Found You

Molly Black

Bestselling author Molly Black is author of the MAYA GRAY FBI suspense thriller series, comprising nine books (and counting); of the RYLIE WOLF FBI suspense thriller series, comprising six books (and counting); of the TAYLOR SAGE FBI suspense thriller series, comprising eight books (and counting); of the KATIE WINTER FBI suspense thriller series, comprising eleven books (and counting); and of the RUBY HUNTER FBI suspense thriller series, comprising three books (and counting).

An avid reader and lifelong fan of the mystery and thriller genres, Molly loves to hear from you, so please feel free to visit www.mollyblackauthor.com to learn more and stay in touch.

BOOKS BY MOLLY BLACK

MAYA GRAY MYSTERY SERIES
GIRL ONE: MURDER (Book #1)
GIRL TWO: TAKEN (Book #2)
GIRL THREE: TRAPPED (Book #3)
GIRL FOUR: LURED (Book #4)
GIRL FIVE: BOUND (Book #5)
GIRL SIX: FORSAKEN (Book #6)
GIRL SEVEN: CRAVED (Book #7)
GIRL EIGHT: HUNTED (Book #8)
GIRL NINE: GONE (Book #9)

RYLIE WOLF FBI SUSPENSE THRILLER
FOUND YOU (Book #1)
CAUGHT YOU (Book #2)
SEE YOU (Book #3)
WANT YOU (Book #4)
TAKE YOU (Book #5)
DARE YOU (Book #6)

TAYLOR SAGE FBI SUSPENSE THRILLER
DON'T LOOK (Book #1)
DON'T BREATHE (Book #2)
DON'T RUN (Book #3)
DON'T FLINCH (Book #4)
DON'T REMEMBER (Book #5)
DON'T TELL (Book #6)
DON'T HIDE (Book #7)
DON'T BLINK (Book #8)

KATIE WINTER FBI SUSPENSE THRILLER
SAVE ME (Book #1)
REACH ME (Book #2)
HIDE ME (Book #3)
BELIEVE ME (Book #4)
HELP ME (Book #5)
FORGET ME (Book #6)
HOLD ME (Book #7)
PROTECT ME (Book #8)

REMEMBER ME (Book #9)
CATCH ME (Book #10)
WATCH ME (Book #11)

RUBY HUNTER FBI SUSPENSE THRILLER
IF I RUN (Book #1)
IF I TELL (Book #2)
IF I LIVE (Book #3)

Printed in Dunstable, United Kingdom

68162763R00097